MISTLETOE
MOCHAS

PATRICIA D. EDDY

FOREWORD

Dear Reader,

Thank you for traveling to Boston for Christmas with Mac and Devan. These two characters are very special to me.

They're so special, that I actually re-released this book in 2018 (four years after it was originally released) because I had to give them just a bit more.

Originally, this story was meant to be part of an anthology. Because of that, I had to stick to a pretty strict word count. But...I always felt like Devan and Mac needed another date. A little bit more time to get to know one another—and for you to get to know them.

Sometimes, authors don't get things perfect the first time around. Maybe we had a pesky word count limit. Maybe we were just having a bad few weeks. Maybe...we just got it wrong.

Well, one of the best parts about being an author? When I get something wrong, I can go back and fix it. So...that's what I did.

Mac and Devan's story hasn't changed. It's just a bit richer now.

You'll see them again. They show up in All Tied Up For New Year's, and they'll probably show up in one of the Away From

Keyboard books too one of these days. I love checking back in with my characters long after their books are done.

Thank you for coming on this journey with me, and I hope you enjoy Mistletoe and Mochas.

Love,

Patricia

1

S weat dripped down his temples, and Mac Fergerson snagged his towel from the arm of the treadmill. But the motion sent a shock of pain through his ribs, and he hissed out a breath, collapsing against the side rail as he fumbled for the stop button.

Six miles. Before...that would have barely winded him. Today...he reached for the bottle of Vicodin he kept in next to the treadmill in his torture chamber—also known as his second bedroom.

Washing the pill down with half a bottle of water, Mac stumbled over to the window and tried to catch his breath. Snow fell steadily, painting the city streets in white.

He ached for a few hours of opioid-induced dozing on his couch, but not until he'd finished his stretching routine—and made coffee.

Throwing a thick towel on the floor, he lowered himself down carefully, with only a single grunt. Sparks raced through his shoulder as he tried to fold his body into child's pose. His left arm protested, and he fell over onto his right side.

It's a damn yoga pose. A resting yoga pose, for fuck's sake.

Didn't matter. His broken body might never be able to truly rest again.

For the three months he'd lived here—the three months he'd been back in Boston—he'd pushed himself to his body's limits. A treadmill, free weights, and a complex set of pulleys and straps he'd bolted to the ceiling's exposed beams let him continue his physical therapy without returning to the VA hospital in Brockton.

After eight months trapped there, he'd never willingly go back if he could avoid it. The mortar attack should have killed him. Instead, it left him scarred and unable to manage one of the easiest fucking yoga poses there was.

The Vicodin started to dull the constant reminder of the worst day of his life, and pushing to his feet, he tried for a deeper breath and stared down at his chest. Thirty-three shards of metal. Hip to shoulder.

The scent of blood and burnt skin invaded his nose. Lying on the copper-stained sand, he'd prayed for death. Until he'd heard Terry scream. Then, despite a punctured lung, severed tendons and muscles, a shattered arm, clavicle, and three ribs, he'd dragged his broken body ten feet and used his right arm and teeth to tie his belt in a tourniquet around his best friend's leg to stop him from bleeding out.

Months trapped in a hospital bed. Then the wheelchair. Crutches. The cane. And only in the past month had he been able to raise his left arm above his shoulder without breaking into a cold sweat from the pain.

Snagging one of the straps hanging from the ceiling, Mac let his body weight stretch his left hip and oblique. He focused his gaze out the window, desperate for a distraction.

Flashing red lights illuminated the pre-dawn streets. A police car rolled to a stop a few blocks away, and a woman with short-chopped, brown curly hair slipped out of a shop and gestured to her window.

None of his business.

His hand gave out, and he sank like a stone, hitting the floor with his bad knee and a string of curses inventive enough to make the most battle-hardened soldier in his unit blush.

Fuck it all. He'd stretch later. He'd earned some coffee. And maybe a nap. Or at least...rest.

Limping out to the kitchen, he flipped on the coffee machine and grimaced as the grinder protested the lack of beans. Dammit. If he wanted his daily dose of caffeine, he'd have to go out and face society.

DEVAN COULDN'T STOP SHAKING. Frustration crawled up her spine, and she hugged herself tightly, trying not to raise her voice at the tall, skinny police officer standing across from her.

Anger faded to a distant memory as she stared at her front window. Twice in three weeks. Her little coffee shop, Artist's Grind, had been her safe haven for three years. Her home—literally—as her apartment was on the second floor. Her last tie to her family. Until someone decided she didn't belong in the neighborhood. The first time, the uncreative bastards splashed a can of red paint all over her door. That had been a bitch to clean up, but she hadn't thought much of it.

Today, though, they'd escalated. "Get out bitch" now covered the etched glass of her front window. Written in that same ugly red paint. Someone wanted her gone. Not the shop. Her.

She snorted at the thought, stamping her feet on the snowy sidewalk. "My family has owned this building for thirty years," she said as the officer scribbled in his notebook. "It used to be an art gallery. My mom...was a painter."

"I'm sorry, Ms. Windsom, but there's nothing I can do but file a report. Have you thought about installing security cameras?" Officer Taylor tucked his logbook into his jacket pocket and offered her a sheepish smile. "This sort of vandalism is common in a city as big as Boston."

"It's the same color paint."

"Is it?" He narrowed his eyes and took a step closer to the graffiti.

Devan pointed to a corner of the door that still held a smear she'd apparently missed three weeks ago. "It has to be the same guy. Or guys."

"Have you had any trouble *inside* the shop?"

"No." Something niggled at the back of her mind. Her half brother. Sylvester wanted to buy the building. But it's not like Devan was going to be scared off by a little vandalism, and Sylvester knew that. Plus, her lawyer was handling the situation.

Officer Taylor shrugged. "I'm sorry, Ms. Windsom, but there's nothing I can do except file the report. You still have the turpentine from the last incident?"

She nodded. Somewhere behind her anger, she understood the cop was doing the best he could. Artist's Grind was one tiny shop in the big city of Boston, and though she wanted the police to do more, minor vandalism wasn't anywhere near as important as the other crimes in the city.

As the cruiser pulled away from the curb, Devan plucked the rag from her apron strings and started to wipe at the window. Smearing the paint into a giant, red blob, she took a step back. That would have to do until this afternoon. At least no one could read the words anymore.

As the sun peeked between the buildings, motion on the quiet street caught her eye. A man dressed in khaki cargo pants, black military-style boots, a tight t-shirt, and a leather jacket wove amid the piles of snow and ice. Devan stared, oddly mesmerized at how he moved.

Shaking her head, she forced her gaze up to his face. Oh, God. Chiseled features, stubble dotting his jaw, lips pressed together in a thin line. And his eyes. A rich brown, filled with anger—and pain, she'd guess. He looked away almost immediately and shoved his hands into his jacket pockets.

"Morning," Devan said as he passed.

"Yeah," he replied, his voice a low growl. But two steps later, he stopped and turned. "You sell coffee."

"Your powers of observation are impressive." Cracking a smile, she gestured to her apron with the steaming coffee cup and "Artist's Grind Coffee Shop" emblazoned across the front.

The man frowned, and the dark dent in his chin deepened. "When were your beans roasted?"

A tingle raced along Devan's skin at his rough voice. Or perhaps she was merely cold. "I have a Guatemalan blend roasted three days ago. Chocolate and spice notes. My Peruvian was roasted Monday, but I only have enough left for today, so if you like the herbal flavors, you'll want to get it now."

Deep-set eyes braced with dark shadows watched her, and his shoulders slumped under the jacket as if he couldn't make his feet move.

Devan pulled open the door and held it for a moment, waiting to see if the sexy stranger would follow. This was *her* neighborhood, and she knew almost everyone. Mornings were almost exclusively for her regulars, and this man was definitely not a regular. Tammy, a double shot latte with no foam, was due in five minutes. Kurt, an Americano with room, would rush in moments later, and Sarah, who never ordered the same drink twice, would follow on Kurt's heels.

"I'm not paying to heat all of the South End. You coming in or not?"

With a curt nod, he followed. After she'd ducked behind the counter, Devan braced her hands on her hips and waited for his order. His gaze took in the room: the winter landscapes hanging from antique picture rails, beeswax candles in a variety of shapes and sizes, wire stands of earrings, necklaces, and rings, and the crystal wine glasses Devan had been eyeing for herself. All made by local artisans. Devan's little mecca drew in more than simply coffee aficionados.

"I don't walk this way often. The sidewalk on Concord's all torn up," he said, almost under his breath. "This is...all yours?"

"Yep." Devan gestured towards the wares. "Well, I don't make anything but the coffee and pastries. The rest...I take on consignment from local artisans. What'll it be?"

"What would you order right now?" he asked her.

You, naked, on a platter.

Devan opened her mouth, then shut it again before she uttered the totally inappropriate—and completely true— thought. Her cheeks heated, and she stammered, "Um, Guatemalan. T-twelve-ounce Americano?"

"Make it sixteen. That'll get me four shots?"

"Y-yes." Devan lived off caffeine. She figured if someone cut her open, coffee would ooze out of her veins. But there weren't a lot of Bostonians who ordered a quad shot. "Name?"

"I'm the only one here." One corner of his mouth twitched, like he was fighting a smile.

The man was so damn sexy. Why couldn't he tell her his name? "You won't be for long."

"But I'll still be the first."

Yes, you are.

The first customer she thought she could fantasize about since she'd opened the shop. The first she'd say yes to if he asked her out. Every few months, a customer came in, took a shining to her, and begged for a date. She always turned them down.

But this guy...she'd jump at the chance to get to know him better. Or just jump him. Unable to look away from the intensity in his brown eyes, she had a vague sense she should be doing something. Anything.

He arched a single brow, and she took a step back. Coffee. That's right. He ordered coffee.

The bell over the door jingled, and Devan shook her head.

"Sorry. That'll be three-fifty. Hey, Tammy. I'll be right with you."
The perky blond lawyer nodded and fished her wallet out of a
ridiculously bright red briefcase.

Mr. Tall, Dark, and Sexy handed her a five. "Keep the
change."

He wandered off into a back corner of the shop and Devan
shook her head. It was time to get down to business, not dream
about a man she'd never seen before—and still technically
hadn't met.

The grinder whirred, and Devan tamped the coffee down,
twisted the brew cup into place, and pulled the various levers to
send just the right amount of pressure through the grounds. She
inhaled deeply as the rich cocoa notes with a hint of blueberry
wafted over her. She loved her job, loved interacting with
customers, and loved how the unique flavors of the beans
changed over the seasons. Another two shots and Dream Guy's
Americano was done.

"Quad Americano," she called out.

The man sidled over to the counter with that tiny hitch in his
step. An injury? She was almost sure of it. Of course, she'd
watched him the whole time he'd toured her shop. "Thank you . .
." He raised his brows in a question.

"Devan."

"Thank you, Devan." He brought the steaming cup to his lips,
inhaled, and slurped a bit of the black gold. Whoever he was, the
man knew his coffee and how to appreciate it. He reached out
and snagged the sharpie from where she'd clipped it to the top of
her apron. With slow, deliberate strokes, he wrote three letters on
his cup and laid the pen on the counter. One final nod and he
turned and walked out.

"Who was that?" Tammy asked. "I'm always the first customer
here. Don't tell me I've got to start getting up even earlier?"

Devan clutched the pen and relished the lingering warmth
from his fingers. "That...was Mac."

2

*M*ac took another long sip of the Americano. Damn. The woman knew her coffee. Mac, on the other hand, couldn't figure out why he'd flirted with her.

Oh shit. He'd *flirted* with her. All five-foot-five inches of luscious curves that even the loose apron couldn't hide. Her silky voice had tumbled out of her heart-shaped mouth and flowed as smooth as the coffee that slid down his throat. And those eyes. Deep brown. An intriguing mix of innocence and something he couldn't put his finger on.

He flexed his free hand, imagining the feel of her curls tangled in his fingers as he angled her head so he could press his lips—

No more.

He had to stop fantasizing about the woman. It didn't matter how good her coffee was. And it was damn good. Few shops in this neighborhood had any inkling how to make a quality cup of coffee. Hell, most of them had those automatic machines that offered a dozen different drinks at the push of a button. He loved this town—as much as he loved anything these days—but its coffee left a lot to be desired.

As he coded himself back into his building and nodded to the security guard, his mind wandered back to the police lights he'd seen from his window this morning. By the time he'd reached her shop, though, the red paint on her window had been half-cleaned off and illegible. But the lines of strain around her eyes and lips hinted at more than a simple prank.

"Just kids," he muttered as the elevator doors *snicked* shut. "Don't get involved."

It didn't occur to him until after he'd collapsed into his armchair and flipped on the morning news that he hadn't made it far enough to buy beans. Dammit. The throbbing pain in his hip flared as he pushed himself to standing, and he groaned. *Fuck it.* A couple of hours horizontal would help. He'd go out later and hit up the Co-op three blocks away.

Or...he could just visit Devan's shop again in the morning. "No." The word scraped over his throat with an edge he hadn't expected. He was damaged goods, and he wouldn't expose anyone to his particular brand of fucked up.

Even if the brief conversation they'd shared had soothed something broken inside him. Something he'd been trying to fix for a very long time.

THE LIGHT SNOWFALL glittered under the street lights as the pain woke him a little after seven. His solitary dinner of cold pizza sat untouched a few feet away, and he'd never made it out to the Co-op.

Every time he'd tried to work up the courage to step outside his door and face society, he'd found another reason to delay. His second physical therapy session. Another shower—where he gave serious thought to rubbing one out as images of Devan swam in his mind. A sudden inspiration that sent him to his sketchbook for two hours—where all he'd managed to draw were her eyes. And a rendition of her shop's sign that he was seriously considering trying to replicate at the metal shop tomorrow.

Mac limped into his bathroom and reached for the Vicodin bottle. His hands shook while twisting the lid, and ten of the pills tumbled over the tiles. "Shit."

Frustration rose with each pill he retrieved. He'd been about to make it a two-pill day. That was unacceptable. He'd meant to be off them by now. Never mind that his doctors told him he'd probably have pain for the rest of his life. He wasn't going to let his body win. Not after seeing the toll addiction had taken on several of the guys he'd been in rehab with. Mac didn't have much left. No family. No close friends. But though he often wondered if the pain was worth it, he didn't want to die. Didn't want to lose anything more than he already had.

He had a rule. No more than two days in a row and *never* more than one pill a day. Shoving the pills back into the cabinet, he opted for a glass of scotch instead. It didn't take the pain away, but the fuzzing of his mind wouldn't last as long. His head would be clear in the morning.

The phone rang as he took his first swallow.

"Terry. What's up, man?" His former CO called him at least once a week. At first, it'd been clear the man had only checked up on him out of obligation, but sometime over the past year, they'd become friends. Terry had lost the lower half of his right leg in the same attack that had nearly taken Mac's life. Despite this, after only three months, Terry had left the hospital with a prosthetic, finished out the remainder of his enlistment on a recruiting tour, and was now looking for a job in Boston.

Next to Terry, Mac felt like a failure. If it weren't for the man's amazing ability to cheer him up when things got low, Mac would have stopped talking to him entirely.

"I got a job." The smooth voice on the other end of the line held a swell of pride.

"Yeah? Where at?" Mac took another sip. He wasn't looking

forward to the rest of this conversation, even though he was fucking proud of Terry for how quickly he'd recovered and gotten his life back.

"I'm workin' for One Fund. Volunteer Coordinator. I start on Monday."

"That's great. How're you doing with the new leg? Giving you any trouble?"

"Nah. I got a retrofit yesterday. The old prosthetic kept getting sweaty when I was on the treadmill, but this one is awesome. I'm trainin' for the marathon. One Fund said they'd comp my registration."

Silence filled the apartment. Mac didn't know what else to say, and he wasn't relishing Terry broaching his favorite subject.

Terry sighed over the line. "Mac, has anything changed with you?"

"Nope."

"Goddammit. Listen, you've got to snap out of this. Do somethin' with the rest of your life! When was the last time you left your apartment?"

"This morning."

"Really?" Surprise roughened Terry's voice. "For more than just a trip to the mailbox?"

"I needed coffee."

Terry snorted. "Going to the grocery store barely counts. Did you talk to anyone? Have any sort of meaningful conversation?"

"I went to a coffee shop," Mac said defensively. "Talked to the owner some. I might go back tomorrow."

"You're kidding me."

"No." He didn't feel like explaining. Or admitting that he'd flirted with Devan. Or that he knew her name. He'd never hear the end of it.

"What about your metal work? Call any galleries?"

"I'm not that good. The...art...it's something to blow off steam. That's all. I'm looking for a job. Haven't found anything I'm interested in yet. I've got enough saved up for another year. So get off my back. You might be Captain America, back from war, but I'm not. I'll do it in my own time and in my own way. I'm proud of you, man. Seriously. You came back from some serious shit and you did it in record time. But I can't."

"Goddammit, Mac. You're a fuckin' genius with the blowtorch. I've seen your pieces. You could make a livin' sellin' that shit."

"Can we change the subject, please?" Mac was about to hang up on the man.

"Fine. What are you doin' for Christmas? My sister's cookin' a huge spread. Goose. Some epic bread puddin', pecan pie. Come up to Vermont with me for the weekend."

Mac ran a hand through his wavy black hair. It had gotten a little long in the eleven months he'd been off active duty. "We had this same discussion at Thanksgiving. I'm not good company. I'd ruin everyone else's Christmas. I'll get Chinese food."

"Be that way. I've got to get up early for PT in the mornin'. Next time you want to talk, *you* call *me*. Make a fuckin' effort and stop feelin' sorry for yourself. You're alive. Act like it."

The line went dead, and Mac fought the urge the throw the phone across the room. But if he did that, he'd have to go to the store the next day for a new one. Stores meant people. And conversation. And pity. He couldn't handle any more pity.

Trudging back to the couch, he grabbed the plate of cold pizza. Netflix would take his mind off of Terry's call. At least...he hoped it would.

* * *

DEVAN SWUNG the large bag of trash into the dumpster, then slammed the lid closed and brushed her hands off on her apron. The life of a small business owner...

She was passionate about coffee. About her customers. The local artisans she worked with. The less glamorous aspects of her job? Cleaning the bathrooms? Taking out the trash? Wiping down the counters after a fourteen-hour day? Not so much. And she could only afford a few hours of part-time help a week in the afternoons.

A few snowflakes dusted her shoulders and hair by the time she slipped back inside her shop. Only another half an hour and she could head upstairs and collapse on the couch with a cup of tea and an hour of mindless television before bed.

As she rounded the corner into the main room, she yelped at the tall, blond man knocking at her locked door. "Go away, Sylvester," Devan snapped at her half brother. "The shop's closed, and I don't have anything to say to you."

"Come on, Devan. Talk to me now, or I'll come back tomorrow during your morning rush." Sylvester crossed his arms over his chest, an expectant look on his thin face.

This is a bad idea.

Her inner voice told her nothing surrounding Sylvester would ever end well, but if he interrupted her morning rush, she'd lose her temper with him and scare off the customers.

"Fine. You have five minutes." She stomped over to the door, unlocked it, and let him in.

Tracking wet, dirty snow all over her clean floors, he strode over to the counter and leaned his hip against the glass. "Looks like you had some problems," he said, gesturing to her window where a few streaks of red paint remained.

With a brief lift of her shoulder, Devan stared him down. "Nothing serious. Kids messing around. What do you want?"

Sylvester shed his sable wool coat and folded it meticulously before setting it on the counter next to her La Marzocco espresso machine. Reaching inside his suit jacket, he withdrew an envelope. "This is a better offer than you'll receive from anyone else. My lawyer tried to talk me out of this much money, but I insisted. We are family, after all."

Snorting, Devan shoved her hands into the pockets of her

apron. "Family? Just because our father had a wife and kid before Mom doesn't make us family. You never once came to Thanksgiving or Christmas dinner, didn't show up for Chris's funeral— hell, you never even asked Dad how he was doing after he *lost his youngest son*."

Sylvester almost looked apologetic for a moment, shock slackening his features. "I know I made some mistakes. But I'm trying to make up for them now. You're all alone here. Don't you want to move out of the city? Somewhere with a yard and more than two tiny bedrooms? Start a family? I can help make that happen."

He waved the envelope at her again, hope coloring his tone. "Just look at the contract. Think about it."

When she didn't move beyond gesturing to the door, he sighed and dropped the offer on the counter, then fiddled with his coat before shaking it out and thrusting his arms into the sleeves. "It was good to see you again, Devan. I hope to hear from you soon."

"You won't. Goodbye, Sylvester."

DESPITE HIS EXHAUSTION, Mac couldn't sleep. Perhaps that horror movie on Netflix hadn't been a good idea. Wandering over to the window, he gazed down the street. A light dusting of snow coated the parked cars and the sidewalks. Devan's shop was still lit up, but as he watched, the light went out, and a parka-clad form emerged, turned, and locked the door behind her.

Even bundled up, her curves stood out. Tucking a fat, leather pouch under her arm, she looked both ways before crossing the street.

Dammit, woman. Don't you know it's stupid to not hide your bank pouch?

A small, local bank made its home four blocks over, and if she were heading there, she'd have to go right by his apartment to make her night drop.

Mac grabbed his coat. He didn't know if he could reach the street in time to catch her, but he was going to try.

DEVAN TIPPED her head up to admire the snowflakes dancing in the streetlights. The temperature had dipped into the low teens, and the entire city was bathed in white. Devan loved winter. Everything was fresh and clean. The light poles boasted holiday garland, and on nights like this, even her vandalism troubles faded away.

After she deposited the night's bankroll, she could tuck herself in on the couch with a blanket and watch *Love Actually*— one of her favorite holiday movies. Next week, she'd rent a car and go out and get herself a stocky Christmas tree for her apartment and a small one for the shop.

"Four days," she told herself. She closed the shop early on Mondays—always light days—and after this week, she needed the break.

"Hey!"

Footsteps slapped on the pavement from behind her, and Devan tensed. Those weren't running shoes, and their owner was heading right for her. Digging into her pocket for her pepper spray, she whirled around. "Stop there!" she yelled, brandishing the bottle.

The man skidded to a halt and lost his balance on a patch of ice, going down with an audible *oof.*

"Who the hell—Mac?" The man crumpled in a heap a few feet away was Mr. Tall, Dark, and Sexy from this morning. "Are you insane?" She kept the pepper spray held aloft. Regardless of how sexy he was, he'd still chased her down after dark.

"Shit," he grunted. His arm wrapped protectively around his

waist, and pain deepened lines around his eyes and lips. "Admittedly, that was not my smartest plan."

"Running after a woman at night? No. Give me one good reason why I shouldn't call the cops on you right now. I've never seen you before today, and now you're chasing me? Stalker much?"

Devan backed up a few steps as Mac awkwardly got to his feet. "I'm not going to hurt you, sweetheart. I live in the apartment building there." He jerked his thumb over his shoulder. "Looked out my window to see you walking alone with a bank pouch. Are you asking for trouble? This isn't Peoria. It's Boston, for fuck's sake. You're a tempting target carrying that thing." He winced as he tried to gesture towards the black leather bag under her arm.

"I've been making this walk every night for three years. Never had a lick of trouble. Also," she said, wagging the bottle of pepper spray in front of his face, "I'm not exactly helpless."

Mac shoved his hands in his pockets. "Never said you were. But you've got to admit you're asking for it. At least put the pouch inside a bag. Or get someone to go with you this late at night."

"The bank's four blocks away. It's not even nine." Anger sharpened her tone. "Go home, Mac."

"No. I'm walking you to the bank. Once you drop off that bullseye you're holding, you're on your own."

A frustrated groan escaped her lips as Devan took off at a quick clip down the icy street. Mac strode after her, the hitch in his step more pronounced than it had been this morning. She cast furtive glances at him as they went. He wasn't staying too close, possibly not wanting her to feel threatened. Or perhaps he'd hurt himself when he fell. "Are you okay?" she asked.

"Fine," he said and quickened his steps.

Hardly. He was hurting. She knew the signs. Her father had dealt with a chronic hip injury for the last ten years of his life. Mac exhibited some of the same behaviors. Even this morning his gait had been uneven. She snorted. "Be that way, then."

They turned down Tremont and made another quick left onto Worcester. Devan hurried over to the bank, entered her code for the drop box, and slid the pouch inside. "There. It's done. Your white knight duties are officially over for the evening." She set off back towards Artist's Grind. Mac watched her for a moment, then followed, his loping steps carrying an odd rhythm as he crunched through the snow.

When they reached Tremont, he caught up with her and touched her arm. "Where are you headed?" Shoulders hunched against the cold and snow, he ran a hand through his hair and dislodged a small tumble of snowflakes. A few more clung to his eyebrows, and Devan had to stop herself from brushing them away.

"I live above the shop."

"Oh."

They walked in silence the rest of the way to Artist's Grind, and Devan pulled out her keys. "Thank you for your sweet but totally unnecessary chivalrous behavior. I open at six. Tomorrow's coffee is on me. For nearly blinding you with pepper spray. Even though you did probably deserve it."

Mac's shocked look put a smile on Devan's face as she slipped into the warmth of her shop.

$\mathcal{S}$ he didn't expect him to show, but at precisely six the next morning, Mac strolled into Artist's Grind. Tight jeans, black combat boots, and that beat-up leather jacket. Tugging the fur-lined bomber off his head, he sent snowflakes tumbling to the floor.

The storm had dumped two feet of snow on the city overnight, and Devan didn't expect many customers today. Mac's appearance left her gawking as he stamped his feet lightly on her door mat before withdrawing a sketchbook from inside his jacket.

"What's that, stalker?" Devan asked with a grin.

"Thought I'd get out of my apartment for a while," he replied, shifting from one foot to another as he scanned the shop. "What's good today?"

"I got a Kenyan in yesterday afternoon. Bright berries and caramel flavors. It's good as a pour-over." She hit the button on her burr grinder when he nodded. "And the cranberry scones are fresh."

"You got a delivery in this weather?" He raised a brow, dropping his sketchbook on a small table next to one of the couches.

"Baked them myself. My kitchen assistant begged off, but I can still whip up a few things."

"Do you sleep?"

"I don't know that word. Is it supposed to mean something to me?" With a wink, she pulled out a plate. "I was up at four. You want both the coffee and the scone?" Mac offered her a ten-dollar bill, but Devan shook her head. "Nope. On me. For last night."

He nodded his thanks and took a seat facing the window. Devan set Pandora to a holiday theme mix, and "All I Want for Christmas is You" came on the air. She hummed along, swinging her hips in time with the music as she prepared cups and brewed Mac's coffee. When it was done, she waltzed over to his table and deposited the scone, the coffee, and a napkin. Her furtive attempt to glance at the sketchpad in his hands backfired when he tugged it back quickly, but not before she'd spied an ornately patterned Christmas tree coming to life on the page. He grunted what might have been a thank you and turned back to stare out the window at the snow.

Well, that was a dismissal if ever she'd seen one. God, the man was infuriating. Sexy as hell, stupidly protective, and hiding something. Many things.

For the next ninety minutes, business picked up, her regulars grumbling about the weather on their way to work. But a little after seven thirty, it was like the entire city disappeared as the snow started up again. Mac and a local writer who often worked at one of the tiny tables were the only two people left.

Devan tried not to watch him frown at the sketchpad. His right hand held the charcoal pencil aloft, a muscle in his jaw ticked, and he rolled his head around. An audible crack made the local author flinch and glare at him. Devan stifled a laugh. She liked the author—an older woman who wrote mysteries—but she was rather high maintenance. She had to have the same seat in the shop every time she came in, and she watched Devan like a hawk while her coffee was brewed.

As Mac worked, and occasionally fixed her with a hard stare she couldn't decipher, Devan brought out a fresh box of holiday cards for one of the display racks. After she'd tidied the bookshelf and dusted the glass candle holders, she noticed Mac's empty plate and cup, so she approached with a smile. "Do you need a refill?"

He shook his head, glancing down at his phone. "Shit. I'm late. Where do you want these?"

"Don't worry about it. I've got them." She grabbed the dishes and carried them to the bus tub. When she turned back around, he was gone. The only evidence he'd ever been there was a subtle indentation on the cushion and a five-dollar tip.

* * *

MAC THREW the twisted piece of metal into the scrap heap. The pain in his shoulder had taken him by surprise mid-weld, and he'd ruined an hour's worth of work in five seconds.

"You can fix that, y'know." The older woman at the next station angled a gaze at the remnants of what was supposed to be a fireplace poker.

"Not worth it, ma'am," he said quietly. "Wasn't anything...really."

She pushed to her feet and shuffled over to the still-steaming poker. Her thick gloves bore years of stains, and she blew a strand of gray hair out of her eyes as she examined the poker. "I've seen you here a fair bit, son."

"Son?"

"If you're going to call me ma'am, I'm going to call you son. Only fair." She winked at him and dropped the poker back onto his vise. "Clamp that down."

"Yes, ma'am." He didn't want to fix his mistake. Hell, he didn't want to fix anything. But...wasn't that the issue? What Terry was always telling him?

With a sigh, he tightened the vise around the poker's mid-section. The handle had bent and half-collapsed, and instead of being a perfect oval, it now resembled some sort of mangled bow.

"Put the heat right here," the woman instructed, pointing to the worst of the folds. After the metal glowed red-hot, she took a pair of pliers, wrapped them around the overheated section and gave a single twist of her wrist. "Now, do the same thing I just did, but on the other side."

Mac accepted the pliers and willed his hands to steady. His shoulder throbbed, but he could overrule the pain. With a second twist, the metal took shape, and he saw exactly what to do next. The woman watched, her hands on her hips, a small smile curving her lips. "There you go, son."

Two more adjustments, and the handle now looked like a twisting pair of ribbons dancing on the air. Loosening the vise, Mac withdrew the poker and held it up to the light.

"Everything can be fixed," the woman said, "if you try hard enough."

"Not everything." Mac turned back to her, and one corner of his mouth threatened to smile. "But this...yeah. Thank you...uh...?"

"Marta." She extended a gloved hand. "I own this place."

Shock stole his manners for a moment until Marta arched a brow and he shook her hand. "Mac. I thought Frank..."

"Frank's my son. And he manages everything around here. But I've been working in this medium for forty years. You need help again, you come find me."

"Thank you, Marta." As she shuffled back to her station, Mac glanced down at the poker. In five minutes, something ugly, mangled, and ruined had become something beautiful. Could he do it again? Make another one just like it?

Gritting his teeth as his hip flared, he limped over to the raw materials bin and withdrew a thick piece of metal. Might as well try.

* * *

DEVAN'S DAY PASSED SLOWLY. Business didn't pick up again until well after four. Now that the Christmas shopping season was drawing to a close, the evenings brought a flurry of shoppers. Tonight, a dozen books, four candles, three pairs of earrings, a necklace, and five packs of holiday cards found buyers, and Devan called Elora, the young woman who designed most of the jewelry Devan carried, to ask her to deliver more stock.

The rest of her evening was spent updating her sales sheets, arranging for weekend deliveries, balancing her books, and organizing her cash and credit card receipts. If business stayed this good, she could afford to pay a professional to install those security cameras Officer Taylor had suggested she buy.

As she was about to head for the bank, she paused at the door. Mac might be overprotective, but he had a point. She grabbed a reusable grocery bag from behind the counter and shoved the leather pouch inside before slipping into the cold December night.

"Holy shit," she yelped when Mac moved out of the shadows beyond the lamppost. "Stalker."

Puffs of steam escaped his full lips, and stubble shadowed his cheeks. With his hands shoved into his pockets, he frowned. "I didn't mean to scare you."

Her insides warmed and trembled, along with her voice. "What the hell are you doing here?"

"Walking you to the bank. Because clearly you don't listen." He fell into step beside her.

"I listen very well, thank you. Did you not see the bag?"

"I don't see anyone with you, and you're punctual to the minute. Ever hear of avoiding predictable routines?"

She couldn't help her snort. "My life requires routines. And I don't need a big strong man to protect me."

"Never said you did. But you need someone. Most thugs aren't going to target two people, but they'll target one."

They lapsed into silence until they arrived at the bank. Devan dropped off the pouch and turned towards Mac. "Who are you?" His brows knit together, and Devan continued. "Your first name is Mac. You appreciate a good cup of coffee. You live in the neighborhood. You're annoyingly overprotective. You can draw. And you've been injured somehow. That's all I know about you."

Shock unhinged his jaw, and his right arm drew across his body, cupping his abdomen protectively. Turning on his heel, he started walking back the way they'd come, and Devan followed. After a block, Mac glanced over at her. "Two can play at this game. Your first name is Devan. You brew a good cup of coffee. Your shop is popular and you're good with people. And you don't think you need anyone."

"Fine. Be that way."

"What way?" His lips quirked with the question.

"Age-old deflection technique. Answer a question with more questions. Well, I'm not afraid to open up. My last name is Windsom. In my small amount of spare time, I like to read thrillers and science fiction. I sing, badly, in the shower. I want to adopt a dog after Christmas. I went to Boston College, then moved to New York, where I worked as a data analyst until my brother died in Iraq a little over three years ago. Then I inherited this building, moved in upstairs, and opened the shop." They'd reached the front door of Artist's Grind. "Your move."

Mac rubbed the back of his neck and looked down at his feet. He opened his mouth, shut it, and shook his head. "Good night, Devan."

Disappointment sank like a stone in her belly, and she stalked back inside the shop, shutting the door firmly behind her. At the last minute, she turned, and watched him limp back down the street. "Good night, Mac."

* * *

MAC LET himself back into his building and cursed the whole way up the stairs. His latest piece mocked him from the kitchen counter. The little Christmas tree was lopsided, but Marta, the metal shop's owner, had offered him $200 for it. Mac had refused. Marta wanted to display it in the shop's window, and despite his success with the fireplace poker, he didn't want anyone to see his fumbling attempts at something...artistic.

He'd started working with metal as therapy. The hospital had access to a shop not too far from Brockton, and he'd started out in his wheelchair, his left arm nearly useless, turning bits of iron into expressions of his anger and frustration. He'd drawn all his life, though largely in secret, and once he'd been able to use both arms and stand for short periods of time, his work had taken on recognizable shapes.

Why had he walked Devan to the bank again? Hell, why had he gone back for coffee this morning?

Because you're fucking lonely.

He stared out the window overlooking her shop. A shadow moved behind the drapes in one of her apartment windows. Something about the woman called to him. She knew pain. A brother killed in combat. Inheriting the building. Her folks were likely gone. She wore no rings. Hadn't mentioned a boyfriend or a husband, and from the way she looked at him, he didn't expect she had a girlfriend or a wife either. He should stay away. She'd be nothing but trouble. If he kept seeing her—even just for coffee—she'd push past his defenses, and he couldn't allow that.

A chill ran through him, and he headed for a hot shower to try to relax his muscles. Staring down at his body as he stripped off his shirt, he grimaced. The staple scars across his left shoulder, the jagged line bisecting his chest from sternum to oblique, and the rough sandpaper patch under his arm weren't exactly turn-ons.

He'd proved that the first time he'd tried to start something with one of the nurses at the hospital. She'd been flirting with him non-stop. Until the day she saw him in PT with his shirt off. The disgust on her face would stick with him for the rest of his life.

He removed the rest of his clothes, balled them up, and shoved them into the hamper. His hip was even worse than his chest. Hell, you could play tic-tac-toe on his skin. His pelvis would never be quite straight again, despite the myriad of exercises he did. The bones had healed, but his hip socket had been severely damaged by the shrapnel, and bone spurs rubbed painfully with every step. The doctors had cleared him to run, whenever he could stand the pain. He pushed himself every day, though whether for health or punishment he was never certain.

Skimming a hand down his six-pack, he shook his head. If only he hadn't volunteered for that extra patrol. A bitter curse flew from his lips. If he hadn't, some other poor schmuck would have been in his shoes. And Terry probably would have been killed. Terry's life was worth all of Mac's pain. His loneliness. Hell, it was worth more. Terry was a good man. He had a family. A sister, two nephews. His father was still alive.

Mac didn't have a wife or kids. His brother and parents were dead. No one counted on him. He'd made some smart investments before he'd enlisted and he had a good nest egg. As long as he found a job sometime next year, he could wallow in his self-pity and continue his reclusive lifestyle.

"No more," he said, glancing back at Devan's building. Tomorrow he'd hit up the Co-op and buy his own damn coffee beans.

4

―――――

*D*evan trudged down the stairs from her apartment over the coffee shop. She'd slept poorly, Sylvester's offer mocking her from her small kitchen table. In the middle of the night, she'd crumpled it up and thrown it away, but even that hadn't been enough. Not until 2:00 a.m. when she'd torn it into tiny pieces and put it down her garbage disposal, did she manage to fall asleep.

Why the hell did he have a hard-on for the building anyway? The South End was a nice neighborhood—despite Sylvester's claim to the contrary—and she knew the real estate was worth a hell of a lot. But Sylvester owned a dozen properties throughout the city. He didn't need one more.

Yawning, she flipped on the gleaming, red espresso machine. "What the hell?" One of the steamer wands was bent at an unnatural angle. "I cleaned you last night and you were fine." She rushed over to the front door, checked the locks, and found everything just as it should have been. The snow on the sidewalk was unmarked after last night's flurries.

"Oh, you little prick," she muttered. Sylvester had put his coat right next to the machine, and when he'd left the night before, he'd spent moment or two gathering his things. "If you think this is going to convince me to sell, you're a complete moron."

Twenty minutes later, Devan was screwing the replacement steamer wand into place as Tammy walked through the door.

"Oh, don't tell me the machine's broken!" Tammy said, a hint of a whine creeping into her voice.

"Not anymore." With a triumphant fist pump, Devan flipped the switch, and the machine started to purr as it warmed up. "Do you have an extra five minutes to spare this morning?"

"Sure. Half the city's still asleep." The blond lawyer leaned a hip against the counter and gestured to the machine. "What happened?"

"My half brother." As Devan brewed Tammy's double-shot latte, she cringed. "Sorry. You don't need to see—or hear—my dirty laundry first thing in the morning."

"Sweetie, my entire life is dealing with dirty laundry." Tammy pulled out her wallet and slid a five-dollar bill onto the counter. "If he broke your espresso machine, he doesn't sound like a very nice guy."

Devan folded the milk into the coffee, creating a small leaf design in the foam. "He's not. But he's harmless. Mostly. Just a jerk. He wants to buy this place and turn it into a hotel or something."

Tammy snapped a lid on the cup and shook her head at Devan's offer of change. "Well, if you need someone to write him a cease and desist letter, you let me know. I'll give you a 'Coffee Goddess' discount."

"Coffee Goddess, huh? I like the sound of that." Devan laughed, but after Tammy left, she sank against the back counter. "Sylvester, you are *not* going to win."

The door blew back open on a gust of wind, and Devan stalked over and shut it with a little more force than necessary, cringing when her little bell tumbled to the ground. "Great. Just great." Another thing she'd have to fix.

She loved her little coffee shop. Her oasis. Her home. But Sylvester was right about one thing. His offer was at least fifty percent more than the building was worth, and though she was managing, she lived with a constant worry that one bad month or major repair—like the plumbing or the electrical in the hundred and fifty-year-old building—would put her out of business.

Retrieving a step stool from the back room, Devan reattached the bell and stared out into the snowy street. This was her home. Not just the coffee shop and the building, but Boston. And she'd do anything to keep it.

* * *

AFTER HER NIGHTLY CLEANING RITUAL, she tallied the day's receipts in her little office, sealed her bank pouch, and tucked it into a black messenger bag. But when she unlocked the door, the street was empty.

Disappointment squeezed her heart. It's not like she *needed* Mac to walk her to the bank. This was a safe neighborhood, and she knew how to take care of herself. But...he was the first interesting man she'd met in a long time, and...what the hell was his problem anyway? A couple of personal questions and he runs away with his tail between his legs?

She snorted. Pining over a guy she'd had all of three conversations with? Stupid.

Then why couldn't she stop herself from staring up at the windows of his apartment building as she passed.

A curtain fluttered, and for a split second, Devan thought she saw Mac peering down at her. But a car passed on the street, distracting her, and when she turned back to the window, he was gone.

"Your loss, Mac," she muttered. "If you'd been braver, maybe we could have had a little fun."

Pulling up the collar on her jacket against the wind, she picked up the pace. The sooner she dropped off the pouch, the sooner she could be back upstairs with a mug of hot cocoa.

5

*M*ac let himself back into his apartment on Monday morning, a set of fireplace tools and three picture frames in a canvas bag slung over his shoulder. He didn't know why he'd brought them home.

Ever since Marta had taught him how to fix his mistakes, he'd become obsessed. Turning plain, dull pieces of metal into recognizable shapes, pieces with...potential.

The phone rang as he set his bag down, and Mac swore under his breath as he recognized the number. "Doc."

"How are you doing, Mac?" Dr. Nickerson's smooth, deep voice shouldn't have grated, but Mac knew why he was calling.

"Fine."

"Ah...Mac, that's not an answer. Pain level?"

Running a hand through his hair, Mac limped over to his living room window and stared down at Devan's coffee shop. "Five out of ten today."

"You're due for a refill on the Vicodin, and I need to see you back here before I sign off on the meds."

As he watched Devan step outside and spread some ice melt on the sidewalk from a festive red bucket, Mac made his decision.

The one he'd been too scared to make for the past eight months. "I don't want a refill. I want off the meds for good."

Dr. Nickerson's sigh carried over the line. "Mac, you know you're going to have pain for the rest of your life."

"No shit. Last time I checked, I lived in this body. Not you." Frustration edged his tone, and he turned away from the tempting view of Devan's heart-shaped ass. "I'm going cold turkey."

"Not a good idea. Listen..." Papers shuffled on the other end of the call, and the doctor hummed for a second. "Come back to Brockton on Wednesday. There's this new protocol we've had some luck with. Let me do an MRI and check your blood work. See if you're a candidate."

"What's the protocol?" Interest piqued Mac's tone, but he was wary. Anything that trapped him in the hospital again for more than a night was off the table.

"Two days. Extra-strength e-stim, a series of cortisone shots paired with stem cell therapy, and some intensive PT and deep tissue massage. It might give you enough relief to ditch the pills. Because a pain level of five is going to wear you down. If we could get you to a three..."

Memories of his months trapped in hospital beds, wheelchairs, and the rehab clinic sent a hard knot twisting in his stomach. But if he could get his pain to a manageable level, maybe he could go back to Artist's Grind and...see Devan again.

"I'll be there."

* * *

DEVAN STIFLED a yawn as she trudged down the stairs on Tuesday morning. For three days, she'd held her breath every time her shop door had opened. And for three nights, she'd walked the streets alone.

Running a hand through her brown curls, she focused on her front window. "Oh my God."

The glass was a spider web of cracks, and "Fuck you!" had been scrawled in red paint on her door.

A tear escaped before the anger took over. "No, fuck you!" she screamed at no one in particular.

Sylvester had to be the one responsible. The idiot probably paid some punk to try to scare her away. The day before, her lawyer had formally rejected yet another offer to buy the building. And just before she'd fallen asleep, Sylvester had called her, and she'd slammed the phone down halfway through his expletive-laced rant.

Police lights flashed in the darkness. At least she wouldn't have to call them. But why were they already here? Devan unlocked her door, stepped out into the cold, dry morning, and gaped.

"I saw them from my window," Mac said, his hands tucked into the pockets of his leather jacket. "They had what looked like a metal pipe. I couldn't see their faces—too far away—but they were burly guys, baseball caps, black jackets, and black shoes. The shorter one spray-painted the door." He turned to Devan, running a jerky hand through his hair. "Are you okay?"

She shivered, though whether from the cold or his voice, she couldn't tell. "Yeah. What are you doing here?"

Mac looked over at Officer Taylor. "Can we take this inside? Devan isn't dressed for the cold."

The fresh-faced cop nodded and held the door open. When Mac's hand pressed to the small of her back, guiding her into the shop, Devan didn't fight her shudder. And this one had nothing to do with air temperature.

"I'll...uh...get coffee going. Mac? Officer? On the house."

With his notebook in hand, Officer Taylor shook his head. "That's okay, ma'am. I'm off shift in an hour and have to catch some Zzzs. Coffee now would be a bad idea. Though, I'm awfully sorry. Smells darn good in here."

Needing something to do with her hands, Devan ducked behind the counter and tugged her apron over her head. She had to start baking if she wanted to have any scones available for the morning rush. "I don't understand," she said, meeting Mac's dark stare. "You...saw them? Were you watching my shop or something?"

"I was on the treadmill. Next to the window."

As Mac shifted on his feet, Devan let her gaze roam up and down his body. A sprinkling of black chest hair peeked out from the open neck of his jacket. He was only wearing running shorts and sneakers, and a long scar ran down the outside of his left knee. Cheeks pinked, sweat dampening the edges of his brow... With his injuries, he ran?

"You didn't hear anything?" Officer Taylor asked, pulling Devan from her thoughts.

She shook her head, unable to look away from Mac, who leaned against the counter. "My bedroom's upstairs on the back side of the building. I ordered some cameras, but the electrician can't install them until next week."

"I'll put them in them today," Mac said.

"I can't let you do that. I can take care of my own—"

"Goddammit, Devan. I'm trying to help. This is serious. What if you'd been down here already? They only left twenty minutes ago. You could have been in plain view when it happened." Strain colored Mac's tone, and he clenched his fists, his hands shaking, until he blew out a deep breath and forced himself to relax. "I'm installing the cameras today. This morning."

"Mac—"

"Don't argue. I'll be back in an hour. Have the cameras ready." Turning to Officer Taylor, he held out his hand. "You have my number. Call me if I can answer any more questions."

"Thanks, Lieutenant Fergerson. I appreciate you calling this in."

"Lieutenant?" Devan asked. "Mac—"

He glared at her, an odd mix of fear and frustration churning in his eyes. "I'm going home to shower and change. Don't touch the window either, Devan. Safety glass or not, you could get hurt."

The chime over the door tinkled as Mac left, and Devan braced her hands on the counter. "That man is maddening," she said under her breath. At least she knew his last name now. Fergerson. That was progress. She turned to Officer Taylor. "He called it in?"

"He said he saw them twenty minutes after he got on the treadmill. Called it in as he ran out the door. He was pacing outside your shop when I got here."

"Why'd you call him lieutenant? Is he law enforcement—"

"Military. Saw his ID when he showed me his driver's license. I never made it out of the enlisted ranks. You respect your superior officers."

Well, that had to be where he'd been injured. Another piece of the puzzle.

"Is there anyone you can think of who might want to cause you trouble?" Officer Taylor flipped a page in his notebook and waited, his pen poised a millimeter above the paper.

"Um...maybe. My half brother might be involved." There. She'd said it. But even as the words escaped on a whisper, she kicked herself. She had no proof.

"That's a serious charge, Ms. Windsom," Office Taylor said. "What's his name? And do you have any evidence?"

Staring down at her feet, Devan said, "Sylvester Rawlings. And...no. But he...he wants this place. Wants me to sell it to him. I've told him no at least a dozen times, but he called to cuss me out last night—again. Every time he contacts me, he offers me more money, and every time I refuse, he gets meaner."

"Define 'meaner.'"

Meeting the officer's gaze, Devan forced strength into her tone. "He told me I was a stupid bitch and I'd regret underestimating him."

"I can run his name, but I doubt we'll find any prints on the window, and without cameras..."

"I know. He may be a jerk, but he's not an idiot. He always stays on the right side of the law. Barely." She didn't want to confess her whole history to Officer Taylor. The failed restraining order after her parents' death, the bitter legal battle over her inheritance. It wasn't worth it. By tonight, she'd have cameras, and after that, maybe there'd be some evidence.

After Office Taylor left, Devan called a glazier in Dorchester who promised same-day window replacement services and set to work cleaning off her door. By the time Mac ambled back, dressed in khaki cargo pants, combat boots, a black T-shirt, and his leather jacket, she'd turned the angry words on her door into a dark red stain.

"Go inside," he said. "I'll take care of this." As he eased the rag from her hand, his warm fingers brushed hers. Callouses roughened the tips, but the rest of his hand was soft. Brown eyes, dark with an emotion she couldn't read met hers. Need, maybe. He didn't smile, but the corner of his mouth tugged a little.

"God, you're maddening. I can clean my own door," she said.

"It's nearly six. You're going to get customers soon and your fingers are turning blue." He stooped for the bucket of cleanser with a quickly stifled grunt. "Get warm."

Devan shrugged. "Have it your way." If he was going to be Mr. Fix-It, she might as well go back inside. And make him coffee.

* * *

MAC WORKED for hours cleaning her door, installing the security cameras inside and outside her shop, and testing the feeds on her laptop behind the counter. The cameras would allow her to see the street and the inside of the shop from the comfort of her living room or even from her phone when she was away.

He rarely spoke. Only quiet questions about the other tenants on the block, blind spots, and her little artists' mecca. Every time he climbed down from the step stool, his limp was a little worse. Around ten, when the morning rush had finished and the shop was quiet, Devan left Mac fiddling with the last camera and went into the back kitchen. She toasted English muffins and fried a couple of eggs along with two sausage patties. Finishing off the sandwiches with slices of Vermont cheddar, she brought the sandwiches out into the shop.

"Come and eat," Devan said, sliding the two plates onto one of the smaller tables. She returned to the kitchen for a large French press pot and set it down on the table with two mugs.

"Thanks." Mac braced his hand on the back of the chair as he sat. His shoulders hunched over the table, and he scrutinized her with his intense gaze. "How many times has this happened?"

"Three. It's been once a week—give or take."

"Got any enemies?" He wiped his hands and took a long drag of his coffee, his eyelids fluttering a bit as he savored the brew.

Devan shrugged. "My half brother." Now that she'd confessed her fears to Officer Taylor, she found it a little easier to talk about. "My father had a fifteen-year-old son when he married my mom. I never really knew Sylvester. He was in college when I was born, and the only time we ever saw him was at Christmas—if he needed money."

"What does he want with the place?"

"To turn it into a boutique hotel. He sued me for the building after my brother died. But I won. Mom and Dad left it to me. It's mine and he's never getting it."

"Sylvester. He got a last name?"

"Mac, you can't—"

"Shit, Devan. You were lucky I saw them when I did. What if I hadn't? What if you'd walked in on them? You could have gotten seriously hurt. Have you told the police what you think?"

"I mentioned him to Officer Taylor this morning. But there won't be any evidence. Sylvester's too smart for that. He's been buying and selling real estate in this town for twenty years. You said it yourself, they were thugs. If Sylvester *is* behind this, he probably found someone he could pay in cash. Untraceable. But he's going to have to work a lot harder than that to scare me. This is my home. I grew up here. My brother lived here. It's mine, and I'm not selling. Not even for the full appraised value of the place. Or more. I don't care what he wants. He never lived here. He doesn't love it like I do. He wants to make money and he thinks this is the way to do it."

Mac's hands clenched and unclenched as she spoke. A muscle in his jaw ticked and he squeezed his eyes shut. When he opened them again, Devan saw pain.

"I can't protect you," he said, almost to himself. Clearing his throat, he straightened his shoulders. "You have to pursue this."

"There's no evidence. No fingerprints. No witnesses. Well, other than you. How early do you get up?" Devan polished off her sandwich and sat back in her chair, watching him carefully.

"Early," he muttered and leaned on the table heavily as he stood. "Thanks for the lunch. You're set up. I have to be some-where in half an hour, but I'm going to walk you to the bank tonight. I'll meet you here at eight."

"Mac, wait." Devan reached out and grabbed his left arm.

With a wince, Mac's entire body went rigid. He swore under his breath, and his eyes flashed, dangerous and full of pain. "Don't touch me there, Devan."

"What happened to you?"

"Not a subject open for discussion. I'll see you at eight."

6

---

*M*ac limped back to his apartment in a foul mood. He'd pushed himself all morning helping Devan, and he'd pay for it for the rest of the day. Reaching up over his head was the one thing he still had trouble with.

The tendons in his shoulder had been almost completely severed. He'd spent four months with his arm immobilized in a sling—and trapped in a wheelchair from all the damage to his hip. When he looked at himself in the mirror, he still thought his shoulders were lopsided. But at least now, Devan would have evidence if those thugs came back.

By the time he'd reached the street this morning, they'd run off. He hadn't lied to her. Just...hadn't told her the whole truth—that he'd been on his treadmill because the pain had woken him up at 4:00 a.m. Or that he'd pushed himself to install the cameras so he could fall into an exhausted heap on his bed and catch a couple of hours. He'd managed three days without the Vicodin so far, and the pain had him constantly on edge. Three days drug-free and three days Devan-free . . . until this morning. The latter made him a hell of a lot crankier than the former, and he was baffled. He barely knew her.

When he was around Devan, he almost forgot about the pain. It never totally left him, but he didn't focus on the constant dull throb with her in the room. If the doc really could help him get off the meds for good, maybe...he could ask her out. Maybe he wouldn't feel so...damaged.

What the hell are you thinking? One look at you and she'd run, screaming.

Or would she? Despite the trouble she'd had, Devan wasn't scared. From the little learned of her in the past week, she didn't take crap from anyone—not even him. Still, he was a fool to think she might be interested in him.

Pulling back the drapes in his living room, he angled a glance down at her shop. A woman with a large canvas tote shouldered her way through the door, and he caught a glimpse of Devan coming to greet her, the two embracing like old friends.

She didn't need him. And she definitely didn't need his damage. No. He'd walk her to the bank because it was the right thing to do, but he wouldn't pursue her. Just do his part to keep her safe.

She's part of the neighborhood. Her shop is cozy, comfortable. I'd miss it if she closed.

It couldn't be that he'd miss *her.* He didn't know Devan well enough to miss her.

Mac unlaced his boots, threw back the blankets on his bed, and curled around his pillow. He'd spent the past three days trying to leave her alone. So what if he hadn't been able to stop himself from watching over her during her nightly bank runs? He had an obligation to the neighborhood, didn't he?

He hadn't gotten involved. Hadn't approached her. He'd peered down from his window, making sure no one gave her any trouble and waited for her to return. Running shoes laced, phone in hand—in case she didn't come back in a reasonable amount of time.

He liked the curvy brunette. She had an easy smile with her customers, a dry sense of humor, and she didn't see him as crippled. Of course, that was before she'd grabbed his arm, and he'd snapped at her. What would she see now? She knew he was hurting. Would she let him be? Or keep pushing? If she pushed, he'd walk away. Never seeing her again would be easier than watching her face twist with disgust at the sight of his body.

Mac punched the pillow with his good arm. "Stop it. You're going to walk her to the bank. Nothing more." He fell asleep trying to convince himself that was all he wanted to do.

* * *

WHEN MAC STEPPED out of his apartment a few minutes before eight, a light, misting rain dampened his hair around his collar. He pulled his jacket tighter. A few hours of fitful sleep hadn't left him with any answers. Or peace.

But as he limped down the street, he realized he didn't care. He wanted Devan. Wanted to know her. But if he let her in, well... she certainly wouldn't stay long. Maybe a few hours...a day...but that might be enough to get him through.

Through what? It's not like your life is ever going to get any better.

"Get over yourself," he muttered under his breath. "Walk her to the bank, then go home."

Artist's Grind glowed with twinkling Christmas lights strung around the newly replaced window. Devan had her back to the door, leaning against the counter with her phone pressed to her ear. He rapped on the glass, and she flinched, turned, and then blew out a breath before motioning him inside.

"Sorry," she whispered. "I'm on the phone with my lawyer." After Mac flipped the lock on the door—why hadn't she locked it when she'd closed?—he watched Devan disappear into a little office down the hall.

This couldn't be good. The quick smile she'd flashed him hadn't reached her eyes, and her shoulders were tense. Mac hovered at the end of the hall, just close enough to hear her voice.

"I don't care what he wants or how much the offer is. How many times do I have to tell you, Oliver? I'm. Not. Selling." Mac took two steps towards the office before Devan continued, "Five million. Shit." After another pause, her voice strengthened. "Well, fuck that. This is my home. He can pry me out of here when I'm cold and dead."

He should go. Or...at least stop listening. But like watching a train wreck, Mac couldn't bring himself to move.

"Did I suddenly forget how to speak English? Or do you really not understand? Geez, Oliver, don't make me regret keeping you on all these years. Dad loved you like a brother, but the past few months, you've been treating me more like a child than a thirty-one-year-old business owner who pays you an insane amount of money per hour. Respond to Sylvester and tell him, yet again, we do *not* have a deal. I'll see you in two weeks so we can take care of next year's permits. But right now, I have to make my bank drop. I'll talk to you later."

Devan stalked out into the main room and reddened when she saw Mac hovering at her front counter. "You didn't need to hear that."

"Five million?"

"Yeah. That's how much Sylvester is apparently in debt. He's getting desperate."

"How did your lawyer find that out?"

"*The Beantown Babbler.*"

"The Babbler's running a story on your half brother?" Mac couldn't help his disbelief. Who the hell was this Sylvester anyway? He'd seen the sensationalist rag at the grocery store a time or two, but never paid attention to anything they "reported."

"Yeah. He owns the old mall down in Watertown. A couple of

housing complexes in Quincy. Three hotels. He's kind of a big deal. Or was. He's been losing money for years now. Ever since the market crashed in 2008."

The hairs on the back of Mac's neck prickled. Money was a powerful motivator. "He thinks this place will get him out of debt?"

Devan shrugged. "It's worth four million. Or close to it. I guess he thinks the money he'd get from opening the hotel would do the rest. Either that, or he's a petty, misogynist asshole who can't stand that his little half sister is moderately successful and he's not. In the past week, he's contacted me three times. Once in person and twice through Oliver. Apparently 'no way in hell' and 'over my dead body' aren't words he understands."

Cursing to himself, Mac shoved his hands into his pockets. Sylvester was escalating. How long before he wouldn't just go after Devan's shop, but would target her?

Despite the pain in his hip, he was fucking glad he'd spent all of the time and effort on the cameras today, and he was sure as hell going to be watching her place at night for the foreseeable future—whenever he could. Worries about his trip to Brockton in the morning weighed him down. He rolled his head around, trying to release the tension gathered between his shoulder blades. "Are you ready?" he asked.

"Oh. Yes. I'm sorry. I shouldn't be dumping all of my frustrations on you." She slid the bank pouch and her wallet into the inner pocket of her rain jacket and gestured towards the door. Mac looked up and down the street, saw only a few casual shoppers and commuters walking from the T station two blocks up, and nodded.

Dump all you want, sweetheart.

Mac waited until she locked the door behind her, and then they set off at a brisk walk through the drizzle. Devan stayed close to his left side, raising his hackles, but it was the safest place for her. If anyone approached them, Mac needed to be able to swing with his right arm.

Devan snuck glances up at him as they made their way down the block. "Why are you here?"

"Because I don't have anything else to do." The words shocked him. It wasn't exactly the truth. He didn't have anywhere else to be *right now*, but even if he'd had obligations, he'd have shirked them. He'd been an officer. Led a team of men for two years in Afghanistan. Protecting people—that was who he was. A piece of him he'd thought long dead—stolen by the attack that almost killed him—flared to life.

Protecting Devan gave him a purpose again.

"No job? You don't look like a trust fund baby," she teased. "Win the lottery?"

"Mortar attack. Afghanistan. A year ago," he said, his voice a hoarse whisper. "Only been out of the hospital for three months."

"God. Mac." Devan stopped in her tracks and waited for him to face her. Worry painted her features with lines he didn't like to see around those bright brown eyes. "That's why you limp a little. Why you don't want me to touch you."

"Yes."

"Dammit, all that work you did for me today hurt you, didn't it?"

"Breathing hurts me, sweetheart. Can we keep walking? It's cold and wet out."

Her mouth opened and closed, and she seemed to struggle for her next words, but finally shook her head and set off—slower this time. As they reached the bank, Mac stayed a few feet away, letting her punch in her code for the drop box. Her ass swayed as she stamped her feet, trying to keep warm. A hat hid her curls, and water dripped from the brim, rolling off her black coat.

After she'd closed the drop box, she turned, her lower lip askew, her eyes shining in the streetlights. "It's late. But can I buy you dinner? Or a drink?"

Not a good idea. Go home. Find something mindless on TV and try to forget about her.

Despite all the excuses he came up with in his head, his mouth had other ideas. "I could eat."

"Good. Pasta okay?"

No. Tell her you've got to go. Walk her home and be done with it.

"Fine."

Devan held out her hand. Mac squeezed his eyes shut for a second. This was going nowhere good. He cleared his throat and forced himself to look at her. She smiled, hope lifting her brows. His body betrayed him when his right arm stuck out to accept her hand in the crook of his elbow.

"This is okay?"

"It's my left side that's messed up."

"Oh."

He could tell she wanted to ask questions. His psychiatrist had told him to open up. Hell, Terry would tell him to throw his good arm around her and kiss her. A deep sigh puffed out his chest. "I don't like talking about it. Hell, this is a mistake. I'm not good company."

"You know," she said, looking up at him and waggling her eyebrows, "people always say that. But how can you tell if you're good company? If I'm enjoying myself, even a little, doesn't that mean you're doing fine?"

He huffed, but he couldn't argue with her logic. Still, what the hell did she see in him?

Devan led them to a little hole-in-the-wall Italian restaurant three blocks from her shop. The tables were covered with the standard red checkered cloths, but in homage to the season, green candles burned next to little bottles of olive oil and balsamic vinegar. When they were seated in a dim corner with glasses of chianti, she stared him down. "You're a puzzle, Mac Fergerson. A handsome, infuriating puzzle."

He nearly choked on his wine. "Infuriating?"

Wait, did she say handsome?

"Yes. Other than the limp, which isn't bad, by the way, you're the best looking man to walk into my shop in three years. Yet you're hiding. From everyone. Do you have any friends?"

"A couple." He leaned back in his chair, his body rigid.

"See them at all?"

"No. Not recently."

"Family?"

"Dead. Brother in Desert Storm, parents not long after that in a car accident." He had to change the subject or he was going to bolt. "Have you always had good taste in coffee?"

She chuckled. "Good deflection. I'll let you get away with it. For now. I lived next to a great shop in New York. They did cuppings every week. Taught me everything I know. I still miss them. Hell, I miss New York. But Boston's my home. Always will be. My brother always said you couldn't get a good bagel in Boston or good cannoli in New York. He was right. And I love both of those things." She cracked a smile, but sadness welled in her gaze.

Mac fiddled with his napkin, twisting the corner in his lap. Why did he suddenly want to know everything about her? He didn't like the way her eyes threatened to water and her shoulders slumped. *Don't go there. Don't risk it.*

Again, his mouth overruled his head. "I want to ask you something, but I don't want to bring up anything traumatic."

Devan rubbed the back of her neck as she picked up the menu. "Land mine. Chris was patrolling, and one of the local kids kicked a ball outside of the safe zone. Chris went to retrieve it. His unit knew where all of the mines were. Well, almost all of the mines. We were twins. Born twelve minutes apart."

"You were older?"

"Yeah. What? Am I that bossy?"

"I'm here, aren't I?" Mac asked with the first genuine smile he'd cracked in longer than he wanted to admit.

"You are." Devan's long fingers curled around her wine glass. "You have a nice smile. I'm glad I finally got to see it."

The waiter showed up with bread and Mac was spared the embarrassment of having to meet her gaze. This was...nice. He'd forgotten what it was like to sit comfortably with someone and talk. Or listen, since Devan did most of the talking.

By the end of the meal, a subtle buzz of warmth enveloped him—the wine hadn't affected him, but he was thoroughly drunk on Devan. How could one person be so...intoxicating? Outgoing, open, with an infectious smile and the cutest laugh he'd ever heard. When the waiter brought the bill, Mac grabbed for it before Devan could get her hand on her wallet.

"No. I asked you out," she protested.

"You can pay next time," he replied. *Next time? What the fuck are you doing?* His brain wasn't happy that he'd committed to a second date. His heart was happy some part of him had apparently considered this a date.

Devan's brown eyes went wide. Had *she* considered it a date? She hadn't. "Fuck." He couldn't stop himself. "I'm sorry. I shouldn't have—"

"When?" she interrupted.

"Huh?"

"I want to make sure you're not going to run off on me again. When can we have another date?" Devan leaned forward, elbows on the table, chin resting on her hands. She looked like the stereotypical kid at the candy store window. All wide-eyed anticipation and joy.

Nerves soured his stomach. Sooner or later, he'd have to walk away from her or let her see the monster he'd become. "You don't take no for an answer, do you?"

"I haven't dated anyone in a long time. I don't meet many eligible guys on my schedule. I'm about to turn into a pumpkin and it's only nine-thirty. If I don't fall in bed by ten, I'll be useless when the alarm goes off at four tomorrow morning. So, no. I don't. And the last time I told you anything about myself, asked anything about you, you disappeared for three days. I want a promise. You tell me when I get to see you again, and I'll let you pay for dinner."

He couldn't. Shouldn't.

Mac's stomach clenched. "I have to go to Brockton tomorrow. I won't be back until late."

"Define late." Devan cocked her head and waited for his answer.

"I don't know, but I won't feel up to going out."

"I could bring you soup. I make a mean chicken noodle."

"Why are you doing this?" He slid some cash into the bill sleeve. Before he could pull his hand away, Devan reached out and twined their fingers. The intimacy of the gesture and the electricity that spread up his arm warmed him. He wanted more of Devan Windsom. A lot more.

"Because I like you. And I think you like me. And it's the holidays. Maybe I want to share them with someone this year."

He couldn't say no to her. Not with her thumb rubbing against his wrist. "Thursday. I'll be at your shop at closing time. We can make your bank drop and you can take me anywhere you want."

* * *

Mac walked her to her back door, and nerves coiled tightly in her stomach the whole time. He'd talked more over dinner than all of their other interactions combined, and she didn't want the night to end.

"Come upstairs?" she asked after she'd unlocked the door.

His gaze hooded, all the earlier openness fading in a single breath. "Not a good idea."

"You keep saying that. You're going to give me a complex." Reaching up, she cupped his cheek, the stubble tickling her palm. "I brew a good cup of tea. No expectations, Mac. I just... don't want to say goodnight yet."

The look on his face said he didn't either, but he stood as if he were rooted to the ground.

Devan's breath escaped in puffs of steam as she waited for an answer she feared would never come. *Take the bull by the horns. If you don't make a move, he's never going to.*

Levering up on her toes, she snaked a hand around the back of his neck and pulled him closer. "Mac," she whispered. "Kiss me."

A low growl rumbled in his throat as he pressed her against her door. Fingers tangled in her hair, and he claimed her mouth, his kiss demanding, rough, and all-consuming. Devan responded in kind, fisting the back of his jacket to hold him in place.

Her knees went weak, and she nipped at his lower lip as she ground against him. With her free hand, she cupped his erection through his khakis, and Mac groaned.

"I...can't," he said, his voice rough. "But, God...Devan..."

"More," she whispered.

When he flicked open the button of her jeans and dipped his fingers under her waistband, she shuddered. And then lost her breath completely as he slipped between her slick folds.

"You're so fucking wet."

His words—and the expert way he worked his fingers—sent her flying towards the edge. It had been so long.

Capturing his mouth with hers, she let herself take, even as he thrust deeper. But when he ground his thumb against her clit, she came apart, shattering, with his name on her lips.

Mac held her until she could stand again, his fingers still buried deep inside her.

"Come...upstairs." The intensity of her release had shocked her, but she needed more. All of him. "I want you...naked."

His entire body went rigid, and he stepped back. But though his eyes had gone dark and unreadable, he sucked his fingers into his mouth, and his lids fluttered closed. When they opened again, sadness welled in his gaze.

"You don't know how badly I want you, Devan," he ground out. "But...I can't. I'm sorry."

Before she could come up with a suitable retort, he'd turned on his heel and limped around the corner, out of sight.

7

*M*ac limped into the rehab clinic with his shoulders up around his ears. God, he hated this place. Hated the memories. The feeling of helplessness. Every single day he'd spent trapped in bed, unable to walk. His first physical therapy sessions when he couldn't manage to even hold a fork.

"Can I help you?" The young male desk attendant smiled as he glanced up at Mac.

"I'm here to see Dr. Nickerson. Mac Fergerson. I have an eleven-thirty appointment."

"Oh. Yes. He asked me to send you to the main treatment center. He'll meet you there." The man smiled and leaned over the desk, gesturing down the hall to Mac's left. "Do you need me to show you the way?"

With a gruff snort, Mac shook his head. "No." He'd walked this hall more than a thousand times. With a walker, a cane, and Bridgett, the overly perky physical therapist who liked to torture him.

As the automatic doors whispered open, Mac took a deep breath. *You can do this. It's just an evaluation.*

But the sights, sounds, and smells of the treatment room

slammed into him, and he braced his hand against the wall. Across from him, a young man with tattoos winding around the remaining part of his lower leg fiddled with a prosthetic. Along the left side of the room, a woman—no older than twenty-two— gripped the parallel bars with white knuckles as she took several hesitant steps. And in the stretching area, an older man dressed in the rehab center's dark gray sweats tried to raise his arm over his head, failed, and kicked a medicine ball in frustration.

"Do squats," Mac said quietly as he hovered on the edge of the mat, unsure where Dr. Nickerson was going to meet him.

The guy turned, lines of frustration and age crinkling around his eyes. "It's my arm that's messed up, kid. Not my legs."

"I know." Loosening the top three buttons of his flannel shirt, Mac showed the guy the scar that angled across his shoulder. "You have two problems. Flexibility and strength. You can't fix both of them at once."

With his right hand, Mac grabbed three jump boxes and stacked them on top of one another. He stood facing one side and gestured for the older vet to take position on the other side. "Use your good hand to get your bad one on the box."

Demonstrating, he put his left hand on top of the boxes and let it rest there until the guy mirrored his movements. "Now squat. Three, four inches at most."

The other man dipped slightly, groaning as his muscles and tendons stretched. "Shit, man. That's..." He grimaced, then straightened. "Hurts like hell, but it could actually work. Ollie, that sadistic asshole, is gonna be amazed next week."

A rough laugh shook Mac's shoulders. "Ollie's still around?"

The guy angled his head across the room. "Torturin' one of the newbies right now. I'm Frank."

Mac skirted the stack of boxes and stuck out his hand. "Mac. Been where you are, Frank. It...gets better."

"I hope so. Can't get much worse."

"Mac. You're right on time. Early, even." Dr. Nickerson hurried over to them. "And you've already met Frank. Great. I was hoping you could show Frank around the metal shop this morning. We got a new guy in this morning, and I'm going to need a couple of hours before I can see you for your eval."

In a heartbeat, Frank's smile vanished, and his green eyes hardened. "Doc?"

"Whoa." Mac took a step back and held up his hands. "You didn't say anything about going back to the metal shop. I was supposed to be in and out in an hour."

"You know how it is. We can't control when the injured show up." Dr. Nickerson touched Mac's right arm. "Do me this favor," he said quietly. "I'll be done with the new guy by two."

"I don't need anyone babysittin' me," Frank snapped. "I'm doin' my PT. Seein' the shrink."

Dr. Nickerson sighed. "Frank, you're never going to be able to work construction again. You know that. Spend the afternoon at the metal shop. I'm sure you'd love a day pass out of here, and I'll sign off if you're with Mac. Otherwise, I could send Ollie over?"

Frank and Mac stared one another down, and after a few moments, Frank grumbled, "Fuckin' A. Fine."

A HALF HOUR LATER, Mac pushed through the doors of the metal shop, Frank shuffling behind him. During the short ride in the center's van, Frank had stared out the window, a blank look on his face. Not even the sun reflecting off the brilliantly white snow cheered him up.

"How long you been trapped in the center?" Mac asked as he gestured to the racks of protective smocks and safety glasses.

"Two months," Frank muttered. He yanked the thick, canvas apron over his head, but he couldn't manage to move his arm enough to tie the straps behind him. "A little help?"

Mac cinched the thick cords, then turned so Frank could

return the favor. These days, he could manage, mostly, but he didn't want Frank to feel any more helpless than he already did.

"I had eight months there." Picking up a couple of pieces of scrap metal, he led Frank to a set of vises across from the forge. "Five of them in a wheelchair. Mortar attack."

Frank swore under his breath, then ran his good hand through his salt and pepper hair. "Building I was in blew up. I fell. Onto a piece of rebar."

Mac winced, then showed Frank how to pick up the scrap, where to heat it, and how to secure it in the vise. "Now, take your hammer and pound the shit out of it."

Two hours later, both men were covered in sweat, but Frank had turned a mangled piece of metal into something that could almost be mistaken for a garden stake.

They hadn't spoken beyond the work, but as Mac held the van door open for Frank, the older man paused. "You're happy, Mac? Bein'...less than you were? Knowin' you'll *always* be less than you were?"

Mac thought for a long minute. Happy? He hadn't been happy since before the attack. Except... for dinner with Devan. For those couple of hours...

"I'm alive. And that's better than the alternative."

IN THE DOC'S exam room, Mac paced. Barefoot, wearing the ridiculously revealing hospital gown that never tied tightly enough. Still jittery from the scans and the contrasting shit they'd injected him with to check his circulation. And worried about Devan. He didn't think he'd be able to walk her to the bank tonight. Not with as late as he was going to get out of here. He should have called someone. Terry would have done it. Dammit. He didn't even have Devan's number. Couldn't call to check up on her.

But...even if could...he shouldn't. She'd get the wrong idea. Or maybe he would.

The quick rap on the door made him hiss out a breath as his shoulder tensed up. "Yeah."

"I'm sorry, Mac. Today's been one crisis after another," Dr. Nickerson said as he rushed into the room. "I have the results of your scans, but I need to do a physical evaluation too. Let's see how that shoulder looks."

Mac yanked on the cotton tie and let the thin gown fall off his left side.

"Arm up."

For a full ten minutes, the doc checked his range of motion, dug his fingers into Mac's soft tissue, and stared at the results from the myriad of scans.

"So?" Mac asked when Dr. Nickerson finished typing up his notes, and Mac had been able to get dressed again.

"You're a candidate for the new protocol. I'm still not sure this is the best timing—" the doc held up his hand when Mac started to protest, "—but if you're serious about working the program, we can give it a shot."

"I'm serious. I want off the meds. For good."

"When was your last dose?" the doctor asked with a frown.

"Four days ago."

The doc's eyebrows shot up, and he crossed his arms over his chest. "Hell, Mac. I can see the pain etched all over your face, and you're just sitting in a chair doing nothing."

With a sigh, Mac muttered, "I feel like I'm about to come out of my skin."

"So why now?" Leaning back, the doc watched him with a critical eye.

Pushing to his feet, Mac started to pace, needing to do something besides let Dr. Nickerson's stare eat away at him. "I hate how the meds make me feel. Like the world's dull and out of focus. Like...nothing matters. I know I'm lucky to be alive. And to be walking. But...it's not enough. I need this, doc."

The older man nodded. "Okay." Tapping a few keys, he brought up his calendar. "Come back on Friday. You'll stay overnight, and ideally, we'll get you out of here on Saturday afternoon. Sunday morning at the latest. But you need to do one thing for me."

Grinding his teeth together, Mac turned to face the doc. "What?"

"When you get home tonight, take your meds. Tomorrow, too. On Friday morning, I want you as pain-free as possible, because when you leave, you're going to be a mess. It'll get better, but I'll warn you now—if you have anyone who can help you out on Saturday when you get home, call 'em."

Though nerves tightened in his gut, Mac forced a smile and offered the doc his hand. "Thanks."

* * *

ALL DAY, Devan's gaze snapped to the door every time the chimes rang, hoping Mac would surprise her and show up. The headache brewing behind her eyes wouldn't go away, and the memory of Mac kissing her, touching her, making her come played on repeat every time she took a break. The feel of him, the sound of his very male growl as he'd tasted the fingers he'd dipped into her panties. But then...he'd walked away, and she had no idea if he was planning on coming back again.

A little after five, Elora rushed in, a small bag dangling from her arm. "I'm sorry, Devan. I wanted to get here before you closed, but the T was packed."

With a weak laugh, Devan angled her head towards the pile of receipts on her counter. "I'll be here another two hours at this rate."

"You really need to hire someone to help you." Elora set the bag down on one of the tables and started unpacking dozens of small boxes. "This is everything I have from my back stock. Ten pairs of earrings, eight pendants, six bracelets, and fifteen rings." Skirting the counter, Devan wrapped Elora in a quick, tight embrace. "Thank you. You're a life saver. I don't know what happened, but the past two days, people have been buying gifts left and right. It's like they just realized Christmas is only ten days away."

The two worked for twenty minutes, Elora arranging her wares and Devan recording inventory numbers and prices for each item. When she'd finished, she ducked into her office for her checkbook.

"Five hundred and sixty," she said with a smile. "Any chance you'll have more for me next week? With how quickly your stuff sells..."

Elora sank into one of the chairs and pinched the bridge of her nose. "I don't know. Working full time and spending every evening making jewelry is exhausting. I haven't been feeling well lately. The headaches..."

Diagnosed with a rare disorder—Sturge-Webber Syndrome —at birth, Elora suffered from seizures, and was half-blind in one eye. Yet Devan had never met such a strong, capable woman, or one as sweet. A few months ago, Elora'd had a seizure in the middle of Devan's shop, and Devan had bundled her in a blanket on her couch for hours until she'd felt strong enough to go home. Since then, their friendship had flourished.

"How close are you to being able to quit for good?" Devan reached under the counter and pulled out a bottle of wine. She poured them each a glass, pulled the shades on the windows, and urged Elora over to one of the super soft leather sofas in the corner.

"You read my mind," Elora said as she toasted Devan. "And I... I want to quit. So badly. Maybe...after the holidays."

"Are you doing anything for Christmas?" Devan asked.

Elora stared down at her hands. "My eye is getting worse. I'm having laser surgery on the twenty-third. So Christmas will be takeout and painkillers, I think."

"I'll bring you soup." Devan wrapped her arm around Elora's shoulders. "You don't have to entertain me. I won't even stay. But you won't be eating takeout—or at least not only takeout—after surgery. Not while I'm around."

After she sniffed and wiped at her watery eyes, Elora took a long sip of her wine, sinking further into the cushions. "What's going on with you?"

Devan groaned. "I met a guy. Sort of." After a long pause, she dropped her head into her hands. "He lives a block away. And he's... oh, God. He's handsome and infuriating and last night..." Her cheeks flushed hot. "Anyway...I don't know if it's going anywhere. He's closed off, and I don't know how to reach him."

Elora drained the last of her wine and ran a hand through her thick, reddish-brown locks. "You're definitely not asking the right person, Devan. My love life..." With a huff, Elora shook her head. "But if you like him...well, I've never known you to be someone who gives up easily."

Laughing—probably more from the wine than Elora's assessment of her—Devan hugged her friend. "I needed to hear that tonight, honey. Thank you. I think we're having another date tomorrow. I'll pin him down. Literally."

"Good. You do that. Now I'm going to go home and see how many more pairs of earrings I can make between now and the end of the weekend."

After she'd locked the door, Devan climbed the stairs and headed for bed, forgetting all about her bank drop.

"*S*hit." Devan dropped a steaming cup of milk on the floor, splattering her jeans, sturdy black shoes, and the cabinets. All day, she'd been a nervous wreck. Hell, after Elora had left last night, she'd stared up at Mac's window before bed, hoping to see a light on. But there'd been no sign of him.

He hadn't come in this morning either. Would he show up for their date tonight? And if not...dammit. She was going to wait outside *his* building like a stalker until she could give him a piece of her mind. The bell over the door jingled, and Devan glanced up from her kneeling position on the floor, rag in hand. "Be with you in a minute."

"Devan Windsom?"

"That's me," she said. "What'll it be?" Pushing to her feet, she brushed her hands off on her apron, then turned to her cash register.

"Nothing." The tall, thin gentleman with an easy smile handed her an envelope. "You've been served. Have a nice day."

As the door slammed shut, Devan shouted, "Bastard!" At least the shop was empty. The poor process server didn't deserve her anger. It wasn't his fault. No. It was Sylvester's. Ripping open the envelope, she glowered at the summons. What the hell was he doing? He'd contested her parents' wills three years ago and he'd lost.

"Defamation of character? The hell?" As she scanned through the documents, she snorted. What an idiot. He actually thought *she'd* been the *Beantown Babbler's* source. "How the hell would I even know your financial information, you stupid jerk?"

"I don't know. Are you secretly a hacker on the side?" Mac stood just inside the door, his hands shoved into his pockets and an odd expression on his face.

Devan's eyes burned until she forced out a deep breath. "I was beginning to worry you wouldn't show up."

His shoulders hiked up around his ears. "I said I would."

Something was off with him. His words were...a little slow. Not quite dull, but without the rough edge she was used to. Dropping the summons, she strode over and wrapped her arms around him. He groaned and stumbled back.

"Devan, be careful."

Shame washed over her as Mac tried to balance. When his back hit the door jamb, he hissed out a breath, and Devan let him go, her hands on his upper arms to steady him. "Oh, God. I'm sorry."

"It's fine," he said through gritted teeth. "I...uh...came by to ask you if we could maybe do drinks instead of dinner tonight. I have an early train to catch in the morning, and I need..." He ran a hand through his hair. "There are some things I need to take care of before I go."

Disappointment raised a lump in Devan's throat, but she forced it away. "Sure. I can close up a little early and make my bank drop by six. Where are you going?"

"Brockton. Two days this time."

"What's there?" Devan slid her hand down his arm, linking their fingers, but Mac barely responded to her touch. His eyes were bloodshot and a little cloudy, and he hadn't shaved. "What's wrong, Mac?"

"Just a bad night. Didn't sleep much." Pulling away, he reached for the door handle. "Six, then?"

As soon as she nodded, he turned and slipped out the door.

* * *

"*You're an asshole,*" he thought as he limped back to his apartment. Hell, he hadn't even asked her what she'd been yelling about when he'd walked in. He hated the drugs. Hated how dull they made his mind. At least this dose would mostly wear off in a couple of hours, and maybe they'd have a passable date. Though why she wanted to date him...he still didn't know.

Mac stared down at her shop from his living room window, wishing he had the courage to tell her he liked her. That he hadn't liked anyone in a long time. Especially not himself. This trip to Brockton would fix him up enough for him to be honest with her. He hoped. And if she saw his scars and ran, well...at least he'd have tried. Right?

Stretching out on his couch, he tried to get comfortable as his latest pieces mocked him from the coffee table. Especially the metal rendering of Devan's sign. And the rose he'd been working on for almost a week now.

As his eyes drifted closed, he hoped he'd have the courage to give it to her.

* * *

By six, Mac felt almost human. He'd shaved, stood under the hot water in the shower until it had run cold, and made sure his eyes were clear and his hands steady.

With the metal rose tucked in his jacket pocket, he headed for Devan's shop. All the lights blazed, and when he tried the door, it was open. *Dammit. She needs to be more careful.* Christmas music poured from the small speakers in the ceiling, but Devan was nowhere to be seen.

"Devan? Sweetheart, are you here?"

"In back!"

He found her hunched over her laptop, frowning, a deep crease between her brows. "You okay?"

"Fine." She waved her hand in his general direction. "I'll be done in just a couple of minutes. Have a seat." Her tone didn't match her words, and Mac came around to the other side of the desk and leaned a hip against the wood as Devan tipped her head up to meet his gaze.

"You're not fine. I meant to ask this afternoon, but..." Reaching out to brush the backs of his knuckles along her jaw, he relished the little shiver that ran through her. "I was an ass."

"Maybe a little." Devan leaned into his touch, her eyelids fluttering closed. "Sylvester's at it again. He's suing me."

Rolling her chair back slightly, Devan spread her knees so Mac could shift and fit himself between them. The position gave him access to her curls, and he twisted his fingers in the soft locks. "Devan, he's escalating. I'm worried about you."

"You made sure I had cameras," she said with a weak grin. "He's an idiot. So's his lawyer, apparently. *The Beantown Babbler* confirmed I wasn't their source. Turns out, when Sylvester tried to get one of his buildings listed on the Boston Register of Historic Places, he had to turn over all of the paperwork surrounding the purchase. Everything the *Babbler* used was public record."

"You're here alone every time I come in. And your door wasn't even locked." Mac leaned down and brushed his lips to hers. God, he'd waited almost forty-eight hours to taste her again, and now that he had, he never wanted to stop.

She leaned into him, her arms wrapping gently around his waist. "I missed you," she murmured when they finally broke off the kiss. "Where'd you go? And where are you going tomorrow? Don't just say Brockton. That doesn't tell me anything."

"I...uh..."

Devan's little gasp saved him from answering, and she jerked back. "What do you have in there? A set of knives?"

He laughed—actually laughed—something he didn't think he'd done in quite a while as he unzipped his jacket and pulled out the metal rose. "Flowers die. This...won't."

"Oh my God. It's beautiful. Where did you find this?" Devan's delicate fingers traced every petal, a look of pure joy and awe smoothing her features. Her brown eyes twinkled when she met his gaze, and heat licked up his cheeks.

"It's...mine. I mean...I made it."

"Mac?" She pushed up so she could grab his right shoulder—his good one—with her free hand. "This is amazing. The detail work. The color. You could sell these."

"It's just a hobby," he protested. "I'm not very good—"

"Bullshit." Devan pressed closer to him, and fuck, he loved the feel of her. How she smelled like coffee and fresh rain. How her breasts felt against the thin fabric of his Henley, her nipples pebbling. "This may be the most beautiful gift anyone's ever given me. Thank you."

Hoping to distract her from any other questions, Mac sealed his lips to hers, his tongue teasing until she opened for him. Cupping the back of her neck, he held her against him, only releasing her when his cock started to press rather painfully against his zipper.

"Mac, you're too mysterious for your own good," Devan murmured when they finally broke off the kiss. "One day, I'm going to learn all of your secrets."

Quickly, he put the desk between them. "Be careful with that, Devan. You might not like what you see."

With a roll of her eyes, she muttered something under her breath, but before his brain could process what she'd said, she snatched up her bank pouch and shoved it into her purse. "Right now, I see a man I want to go have a drink with. You ready?"

He nodded, but worry sat like a stone in his gut. How much longer until she'd see all of him—and run?

* * *

STARS TWINKLED in the clear night sky, and holiday shoppers and commuters crowded the sidewalk. A businessman in a long, black coat bumped into Devan, and she stumbled, but Mac banded an arm around her waist and held her steady. "Hey, jerk. Apologize to the woman," he snapped, but the businessman just extended a middle finger as he rushed down the street. "Fucker."

"I'm okay," Devan said, relishing the way he smelled. Fresh and clean, kind of like the countryside after a storm with a hint of sandalwood. "But this is nice."

Mac dropped his arm and took a step away. "The temperature's dropping fast. Make your drop and let's go somewhere warm."

If he was going to back away every time she tried to get close to him, this relationship—if it even was a relationship—was doomed. And dammit. Devan wanted this. Wanted *him*.

"Yes, sir, Mr. Overprotective," she said, her voice a little sharper than she'd intended. Mac grumbled something under his breath, but Devan stalked across the street to the bank, leaving him sputtering on the curb.

He caught up as the pouch tumbled down the chute. Turning, Devan jammed her hands on her hips. "Where to now?"

Mac frowned and offered Devan his arm. "I don't know any good bars in the area. I don't...get out much."

She rolled her eyes. "I go to bed at 9:00 p.m., remember? But one of my regulars mentioned a new speakeasy around here. One block west, I think."

As they walked, Mac's limp worse than ever, Devan tried to

work up the courage to press him for answers. "I told you about Sylvester and the lawsuit," she said as they turned the corner. "Your turn. What was wrong this afternoon? You were...kind of out of it."

"Didn't sleep last night."

Something in his tone told her that wasn't the truth. At least not all of it. "Mac, talk to me."

His entire body stiffened, and he blew out a breath. "Pain meds...can make me a little...fuzzy."

That single admission seemed to deflate him, and Devan squeezed his bicep. "Did you think I'd...judge you or something?"

"I don't like taking them. Can we change the subject?" Mac's shoulders hiked up as Devan stopped at a door with a swirling metallic symbol at eye-level. She knocked twice, and the symbol twisted, opening enough to reveal an unsmiling face.

"Password?"

"Um...'Wicked Awesome'?"

The door opened, and a petite woman in black pants, a black shirt, and a red tie smiled warmly. "Welcome to Old Fashioned Underground," she said. "Table for two?"

9

Mac fiddled with the cuff of his sleeve. At least the speakeasy was dimly lit. Devan was going to push him to open up, and his nerves were stretched so tight, he feared he'd snap and hurt Devan in the process.

"To a third date?" Devan said as she held her old fashioned aloft.

His drink threatened to slosh over the rim, but he toasted her, his smile shockingly not forced. He wanted a third date. And a fourth. But only if he could get off the meds. For fuck's sake, he hadn't even asked her how she was this afternoon, and he'd *known* she was having a bad day. Felt it in his bones.

"So, tell me about the rose," she said. "What else do you make?"

"Fireplace tools, picture frames, Christmas trees, signs..." He stared into his bourbon, swirling the alcohol around in the glass. "It's just...a hobby."

"Well, your hobby would sell like hotcakes in my shop. Will you show me some of your other pieces?"

"I..." *Find something else to talk about. Now, soldier!* He scrambled for another subject, any subject. Anything safe. "Are the cameras working?"

"Deflecting again." She took a healthy sip of her drink and sighed. "They're fine. Great, even. I check them every morning before I come downstairs. And...no vandalism since you put them in." With a frown, Devan leaned forward and linked their fingers. "Mac, what's in Brockton?"

"Nothing good."

"So tell me. I won't bite. Or judge you. I told you about Sylvester. About Chris." Her eyes glistened, and he felt a slight tremble in her fingers. "I like you. And...I think you like me too. Why won't you let me in?"

Moment of truth. If he opened up now, he'd lose her before what would likely be two days of hell. But if he didn't...would she be waiting when he got back?

"Rehab clinic," he whispered. "I...have to go every few months. Get checked out."

Her fingers tightened on his. "You're scared—"

"Please, Devan. I can't...not tonight. Ask me about my childhood, movies, TV, books...just not this. Not before—"

Before he could finish his sentence, Devan braced her hands on the table, leaned over, and kissed him. Shocked, he didn't even breathe until she pulled away, leaving the taste of her on his lips.

"Trust me, Mac," she said, her face still close enough to his that her breath tickled his cheek. "Trust me to be patient. You don't have to tell me everything. Just don't shut me out completely."

He could only nod as she sat back down, and hope flared somewhere deep inside his heart. Maybe...this could all work out.

* * *

AFTER HE'D LET Devan pay for their drinks, Mac walked her back to her shop and waited for her to unlock the door. He ached to kiss her again—to run his hands down her back and cup her ass, to feel her pressed against him. To do more. "I won't see you tomorrow morning before I leave," he said, his voice gruff and strained.

Devan rose up on her toes and wound her hands around Mac's neck. She pulled him in, closed her eyes, and kissed him. As her tongue traced the seam of his lips, seeking entrance, he obliged without question. She tasted of rye, smelled like coffee and orange blossoms, and was soft against the hard length of his body.

He snaked an arm around her back, drawing her closer. His cock throbbed with a need he hadn't let himself feel in more than two years. Not since his last furlough. Maybe not even then.

His groan vibrated through their kiss. Stumbling through the door, Mac paused only long enough to flip the lock before backing Devan against the counter. Grabbing her waist, he lifted her up, allowing her to wrap her legs around his body. One of her thighs rested against a particularly painful area of his hip, but he didn't care. Not willing to put more than an inch of space between them, he shifted slightly to unzip her rain jacket and cup one of her breasts. It was heavy in his hand, her nipple jutting firmly through her silky, dark green shirt. The position afforded Mac a delicious view of the creamy skin at her shoulder. One button. Two. Three, and her blouse slipped to the side, exposing a black lace bra strap.

Mac nibbled along the corner of her mouth, to her jaw, and down her neck. Her pulse thrummed under his lips. God, she smelled so fucking good. Devan shifted under his hands, giving him better access to her breasts. She squeezed his waist with her thighs, and he felt his balls tighten. Fuck. If he couldn't have her in the next few minutes, he'd come in his pants.

"Back room. Now," she demanded.

He pulled away, his eyes dark with need, and his breath

coming in ragged gasps. "Devan. We can't. I can't. I want to. But I can't."

The look on her face stabbed him through the heart. Hurt and confusion and worry. "Mac..."

The single word was filled with so much emotion. He couldn't leave, couldn't go to Brockton without knowing. Without showing her how much he needed her. "Fuck it."

He cupped her ass, lifted her against him, and hauled her up so she could hang on to his neck. Lurching down the hall, he found Devan's office. Dark, which suited him fine. This way... maybe she wouldn't see his scars. In the dim light from the hall, he searched out the button on her jeans, then with shaking hands, eased the denim—along with her black lace panties— down her hips.

"Mac." Devan reached for his belt, but he took her hands and pinned them at her sides.

"Brace yourself, sweetheart." Unzipping his khakis enough to let his cock spring free of his boxers, he groaned. This was a bad idea. But he could fuck her without undressing. This once, he'd let himself feel. Let himself find release in a warm and willing woman who didn't know what he looked like under his clothes.

Shit.

"Protection."

"Hang on." Devan leaned back on the desk, her chest heaving, lips swollen and glistening, eyes half-lidded. Digging into her purse, she swore under her breath once, then came away with a condom, tossing it at him. Mac had it rolled over his hard length in a single breath.

"You smell like heaven," he murmured as he dipped two fingers inside her and swirled around her wetness. "And you taste like rain."

When he replaced his fingers with his cock, she moaned, and her breath caught in her throat. "Oh, God. Too long," she gasped. "You feel so good."

Reaching between them, he flicked a thumb over her clit, making her entire body shudder. "You're tight. Gotta go slow."

"I won't...break."

Maybe not, but Mac feared he might. After tonight, could he ever walk away from her? He thrust deeper, and Devan's fingers dug into his ass. A second stroke had her tightening her grip, the tiny pinpricks of pain only increasing his arousal and the all-consuming need he had for this woman.

Devan's computer keyboard shimmied off the desk and onto the chair with a crash. Mac grabbed a fistful of brown curls and tipped her head back. He'd dreamed of this. Every night since he'd first met her. "Please," she said, whimpering quietly. Mac sucked his fingers of his other hand, tasting the woman wrapped around him. He wanted all of her. Wanted to bury himself inside of her, tongue probing, and feel her release grab him and pull him into the abyss.

A tingle started in his balls, tightened, and shot towards his cock. His thumb found Devan's clit again, pressed and swirled, and Devan's entire body convulsed in his arms. "Mac!"

Her plaintive cry sent him over the edge with her. Mac came with a groan and pulled Devan against him, holding her as close as he could. They were one, and for a brief moment, he no longer felt alone.

* * *

MAC HELD her for so long that Devan wasn't sure he was ever going to let her go. And she didn't care. She felt safe and protected in his arms, and there was something about his desperate grip that told her he needed this. "Stay," she whispered.

His entire body went rigid. "I can't."

"Why not?"

Mac rubbed the back of his neck and wouldn't meet her eyes.

Devan wasn't sure why she'd suddenly made him so uncomfortable, but she wanted to put him at ease again. "I don't blame you," she said. "Four in the morning isn't a fun time to get up. Will you at least call me when you get to Brockton?"

"No. I can't—no." He let her go, tossed the condom into the trash, and pulled up his khakis. "I have to go. Promise me you won't walk to the bank alone at night while I'm gone."

"Mac."

"Promise me, Devan," he growled. "Otherwise I'm going to worry about you and I can't do that tomorrow. Not where I'm going."

"I'm not a child. Or some sort of pet project. I'm a grown woman and I can take care of myself, thank you very much." Devan tugged up her jeans and slid off the desk. She wasn't going to indulge his stupid alpha male bullshit. She grabbed Mac by the wrist and pulled him out into the front room before releasing him. "Be safe tomorrow, Mac. And...maybe...when you come back...you'll talk to me. Because I can't keep doing this if you won't."

Mac's brows drew together. He opened his mouth, closed it, and balled his hands into fists. "Good night, Devan. I'm...sorry."

10

*D*evan tossed and turned all night. Thoughts of Mac in pain consumed her, and she woke more than once with his name on her lips. Their coupling had been...amazing. But he'd bolted with hardly a word.

With no way to contact him, she worried most of the day. It didn't help that Sylvester had called her ten minutes before closing to read her the riot act for getting his lawsuit dismissed.

On edge, she locked up early, worked on her books, and tried not to think about Mac. Precisely ten minutes before eight, four short raps on her front door had her running out of the office.

"Mac?" Except the dark-haired man standing outside her door wasn't Mac. Devan's smile fell away. "We're closed," she called through the glass.

"Devan Windsom? My name is Terry. I'm a friend of Mac's."

Anger bristled along her spine. Had he really sent someone to check up on her? The nerve. Especially after he'd walked out on her the previous night. "A friend? Mac has...friends?"

Terry laughed, a big, rolling sound accompanied by a wide smile. "I was his CO. Tryin' to be his friend. Sometimes he lets me."

Devan snorted and unlocked the door. She probably shouldn't have, but the man obviously knew Mac. And with the cameras recording everything, she felt reasonably safe. Something about Terry screamed honorable. He carried himself like her brother had. Like Mac. He ambled into her shop with a nod and unzipped his parka before offering her his hand.

His fingers were warm and soft. "Thank you, darlin'. Mac wanted me to walk you to the bank. Make sure you were okay—that you hadn't had any more trouble."

"He ought to be careful there," Devan said, tucking her bank pouch into the pocket of her coat. "He's going to give me the idea he cares."

Terry's black eyebrows shot up, and he chuckled. "He does."

"Well, he's got a funny way of showing it. He walked out without a backwards glance last night after...well...*things*...and I haven't heard from him since. A woman doesn't expect a man she...cares for...to do that to her."

Terry held the door open for her, and Devan's cheeks flushed. Why was she confessing all of this to someone she'd only just met?

Holding out his arm, Terry waited for Devan to tuck her hand in the crook of his elbow before setting out. His steps were a little uneven. Not like Mac's gait. More...loping. Smoother. "Did he tell you where he was goin' today?"

"He said Brockton. The rehab clinic. I tried to ask him to elaborate, but he clammed up and half-begged me not to push him."

"I'm surprised he told you that much." Terry looked up and down the street as they turned the corner, then sighed and patted Devan's hand. "I reckon about now he's in so much pain he can't think straight."

"What the hell is he doing there? Why is he in pain?" Her heart squeezed, and her voice cracked as the haunted look in Mac's eyes flashed through her mind.

"He's in pain every damn day, darlin'. Has been since it

happened. His doc's trying an experimental new therapy that might let him kick the Vicodin for good. He hates the drugs."

"He told me that much." Devan stared down at her feet as they trudged through the snow. Why hadn't Mac confided more in her? She shouldn't have to learn all of this from his CO. Not if they were going to make things work.

"He's tryin' to find a way to manage his pain enough to be done with the drugs for good. Hell, he managed four days in a row without it last week. Probably half because of you. Because he had something to take him out of his own misery. But it cost him. He hasn't slept more than a couple hours at a time since it happened."

Devan stopped, staring up at Terry. The man was easily six-foot-four and built like a tank. "What happened? He only told me it was a mortar attack."

"That's Mac's story. I told you too much already, but he's been a mess since he got hurt. It didn't help that I got my shit together pretty quickly after the attack took my leg. He wasn't so lucky."

"Most people wouldn't call losing your leg lucky."

Terry chuckled. "No, probably not, but I lived. And I do pretty well. Could you tell?"

"I wondered if you'd been injured. But I wasn't sure." They started off again, and when they reached the bank, Terry crossed his arms over his chest, keeping watch while Devan made her deposit.

As Terry offered her his arm again, he patted her hand. "Give him a chance, darlin'. He spent eight months in the hospital. Checked himself out against doctor's orders and didn't want to see anyone. He only left his apartment for groceries or doctor appointments. Pretty sure the only time he talked to another soul was when I called him. And then he told me about this coffee shop he found. And the gorgeous, smart barista who brewed the best cup of coffee he'd ever had. Hell, *he* called *me* last night. Mac

Fergerson doesn't reach out to anyone. Something's changed. I gotta think it might be you."

"Can I ask a favor?" Devan looked up at Terry as they turned the corner onto her block, chewing on her lip while she waited for his reply.

"Mac would kick my ass if I said no. Plus, I don't refuse beautiful women anythin' if I can help it."

"Will you give me his phone number? I won't bother him. One text message to tell him I'm thinking about him."

"No, darlin'. I don't think I should." Devan's face fell. "He's not in a good place right now. But if he calls me, I'll give him your number. That do well enough for you?"

Devan stopped at her shop's door, keys in hand. "It's something. Thanks, Terry. For the company and the insight."

"I'll be back tomorrow night to walk you to the bank. I owe Mac everything. He's the reason I lost a leg and not my life. So when he asks me for a favor, I do it." Terry took Devan's hand and brought it to his lips. "It was a pleasure, Devan."

* * *

MAC'S ENTIRE BODY ACHED. He would have shifted in the thin, hard hospital bed if he hadn't been hooked up to an IV and heart rate monitor. Dr. Nickerson had shown up an hour ago and given him his test results.

Severe anemia plus an allergy to the homeopathic steroid they'd injected in a dozen locations from his shoulder all the way to his knee. Twenty minutes after the shots, his heart rate had shot up to one-sixty, and he'd passed out.

Now, pumped full of Dilaudid, he was nearly pain free. But he couldn't feel his fingers and toes. Fucking doctors. This had been a mistake. A huge, fucking mistake.

After a knock, Dr. Nickerson poked his head into the room. "Mac? How are you doing?"

"How do you think?" he spat. His hand shook as he tried to raise the angle of the bed. "Shit. I need to get out of here."

The doctor shook his head as he tapped his tablet screen. "Until you're stable, you're staying put. You had a critical build-up of myoglobin. Happens when your muscles start to break down. If we don't clear it, you're risking acute kidney failure."

"Fuck. How long?"

"Depends on you, Mac. But if you check out now, you're not only risking more pain. You could die."

Mac closed his eyes, the exhaustion pressing down on him until he couldn't think straight. "Tomorrow," he murmured as he drifted off. "Need to go home tomorrow."

"We'll see."

When he next opened his eyes a few hours later, he focused on the plastic Christmas tree next to his bed, scowling. His thoughts muddled, wandering to Devan. He wanted to hear her voice. Even in the sterile room, her scent lingered in his memory. Her smile. The way she'd linked their fingers, offering him support even though he'd been an ass. And then... their last few minutes together. Her whimpers as he'd tweaked her clit, the feel of her breast in his hand, the taste of her.

He worried about her, and unable to even get out of bed without help, he reached for his phone and called Terry.

"Mac. How are you doin'?"

Open up.

"The shots jacked me up. I...shit, man. I don't know if I'm going to get out of here tomorrow. The doc..." His voice faltered, and he balled his free hand into a fist, using the pain to help him focus. "I'm in bad shape."

"What do you need?"

"Nothing. I don't want to talk about me." *Tell him, you stupid ass.*

But Terry was damn perceptive. "She's fine, Mac. No trouble

at her shop. She's confused and hurt, and I think she's pretty much fallen for you."

Relief—and the drugs—loosened his muscles and his tongue. "I'm falling for her too," he said quietly.

Terry's *whoop* made Mac cringe. "This is a hospital, man. Keep it down."

"It's about damn time," Terry said. "I have her number. If you want it."

Hell yes, he wanted it. But he didn't know what to say to her. And as hopped up on the Dilaudid as he was, he could barely focus. "Yeah. I do."

It took him three tries to save it in his phone, but when he was done, he blew out a breath. "Thanks, Terry. I...owe you one."

"You don't owe me a thing, Lieutenant. Other than to get yourself well enough to get out of there. I'll walk Devan to the bank tomorrow, but I've got plans on Saturday. You've got to be back here by then. You copy?"

"Yes, sir." If he had to pummel Dr. Nickerson within an inch of his life, he'd get out of this bed tomorrow.

After Terry hung up, Mac stared at his phone for what felt like an hour. Devan's number taunted him. He ached to hear her voice. To tell her he cared. To apologize for running out on her.

"Fuck it," he muttered as he jabbed the call button.

"Hello?" Her voice was sleepy and thick, confusion evident at the unknown number and the late hour.

"Devan." He cleared his throat. "Um, it's—"

"Mac. Are you okay?" Rustling carried over the line, and after a long pause, she sighed. "Talk to me."

He didn't know how to answer her. Everything hurt. The room spun around him every time he moved. And he was terrified he wouldn't be discharged tomorrow. If he wasn't careful, he'd say something he couldn't take back.

"I shouldn't have run out on you last night."

"No. You shouldn't have. But you didn't answer my question. How are you?"

"Don't ask me that sweetheart. I don't want to lie to you."

"Then don't." Her little huff had the corner of his mouth twitching up in a half smile. "And don't make me wait all night. You know I have to be up at four."

"I'm better now." He didn't know what else to say, but even listening to her breathing calmed him.

"What's that beeping?"

"Heart rate monitor. Things didn't go well today."

"Shit, Mac. Define 'didn't go well.'"

The lump in his throat swelled at the concern lacing her tone. "Too much to explain...over the phone. I'm...tired, Devan."

"Let me bring you dinner tomorrow. I won't stay long."

"No."

Frustration sharpened her next words. "Why did you call, then? If all you're going to do is shut me out, why even call?"

"I'm not trying to shut you out. I haven't wanted to talk to another human being in a year. Not until you. I called because I missed you. Because I hurt you by walking out and I feel like shit for it."

"Then why did you do it? I wasn't asking you to marry me. Just stay the night."

Could he tell her his biggest fear? That she'd take one look at him and never want to see him again? He didn't think she was that shallow, not really. Fear wasn't logical. It didn't listen to the rational mind. He'd learned that much from his therapy.

"There's a lot you need to know about me, Devan. I can't...not over the phone. I need a little time. Don't give up on me?"

"You'll come on Saturday?" Her brusque tone was almost professional, perfunctory, but the barest hint of a wobble gave her away, and Mac wasn't sure his heart could take it if he made her cry.

"I'll be there when you open." A spasm in his left arm had

him stifling a groan, and the heart rate monitor ticked up even higher. The room started to spin. "Good night, Devan," he slurred, and as the phone slipped from his hand, he heart her sniffle.

"Good night, Mac."

11

*L*ate the next evening, Mac limped up the stairs of his building, using the railing for support. His heart rate was still slightly elevated, but his kidney function was normal, and Dr. Nickerson discharged him with strict orders to get plenty of fluids, rest, and call if he got dizzy.

The argument had taken two hours, but by the end, the doc agreed he could try going off the Vicodin. So now, with a prescription for weekly massages and a gentler anti-inflammatory with no mental side effects, he could try to court Devan.

Darkness blanketed the city, and a light snowfall dusted the streets. He'd thought about ringing the bell for Devan's apartment, but he couldn't see her like this. He needed a night in his own bed, pizza, beer, and some mindless crime drama to settle him. The physical therapy they'd put him through today had brought him to tears more than once.

He was stronger now than he'd been before the attack with an eight-pack any man would envy...if it weren't for the scars spreading from his shoulder to his pelvis. So what if he could curl sixty pounds with his right arm and only forty-five with his left? If he could press a buck-fifty with his right leg and only a hundred with his left? He was doing okay.

His left leg gave out two steps from the top. Well, mostly okay. He clawed his way up to standing and made it to his apartment, panting, and almost stumbled over a brown paper bag in front of his door with his name on it.

"What the hell?"

With a groan, he leaned down and opened the bag. A note rested on the top of an insulated pouch.

Mac, I bribed your doorman with a soup container of his own to leave this at your door. I hope it makes you feel better. —Devan

He swallowed over the lump in his throat. It had been a long time since someone had cared enough to try to take care of him. He unzipped the insulated pouch. A couple of ice packs were nestled around a large plastic container of cold soup. With the pouch under his arm, he let himself into his apartment. He should text her. Or call. Something. But his stomach growled, and his head started to pound. Not yet.

He limped over to the window to see if the lights were on in Devan's shop. No. But the windows of her apartment glowed. Good. She was home and safe. He could relax.

After a beer, two bowls of the best soup he'd ever had, and four hours of dozing in his recliner, he woke up with a start. "Stupid," he grumbled to himself, getting to his feet and rubbing the back of his neck. He'd pay for that uncomfortable nap later. His entire body ached, and his skin was still on fire from the e-stim machine that had sent an electrical current through his muscles when he couldn't manage one more exercise. He hated that damn machine.

The clock on his stove glowed brightly. One thirty in the morning. Great. He passed by the front window before he headed to bed and paused. "Oh shit. Goddammit!"

Two black-clad thugs stood in front of Devan's shop with duffel bags, furtively checking the street around them.

Mac ran.

* * *

DEVAN COULDN'T SLEEP. She'd spent half the day filling out paperwork for a new restraining order against Sylvester. Her lawyer would file on Monday, and maybe that would bring her some peace.

He'd called earlier that day, yelling at her as she held the phone away from her ear.

"Devan, listen to reason. You can't possibly take care of the property like I can. You're going to sink so much money into the building, it'll ruin you. I can have the whole place converted into a vacation rental property in three months. It'll bring in a fortune. I'll even cut you in for five percent of the profits."

Seething, she'd turned her back on a line of customers and lowered her voice, a deadly calm infusing her every word. "My mother bought this building before she married Dad. Their will left it to me, and the courts already ruled you had no claim to it. Find another building to save your sorry ass." She'd hung up on him and closed the shop early. Then she made herself an Irish coffee and curled up on her couch with Christmas music playing and her tree lit up and twinkling.

Now, she thumbed through her recent calls until she reached Mac's number. Had he tried the soup? Or...even made it home? He'd sounded so...unsure when they'd talked, and she ached to hear his voice. But she wouldn't call him. Plus, at 1:30 a.m., he'd be asleep.

Trudging into her kitchen, she pulled down a tin of chamomile tea. As the floral scent infused her apartment, she heard an odd sound from downstairs, and scrambled for her phone to check the camera feeds.

"Shit!"

Two men wearing ski masks and black knit caps were at her

door with a crowbar. The taller one wedged the metal between the door and the wood molding and tried to bust the lock. Devan didn't think.

Racing down the back stairs, she grabbed the baseball bat she kept by the door, and burst into the alley behind the building. Her thin pajamas, robe, and fuzzy purple slippers didn't offer her much protection against the frigid cold, but she didn't care. This was her home and no piece-of-shit thug was going to take it from her.

"Get the fuck away from my shop!" she yelled when she rounded the corner, wielding the bat like a major league slugger. She connected with the shorter thug's arm, her high school softball experience coming back to her in a rush. The man cursed and stumbled back, a duffel bag falling from his shoulder.

Taking aim at the larger guy, Devan planted her foot and started to swing, but her slipper landed on a patch of ice, and she went down on her ass, losing her hold on the bat and sending it rolling ten feet away. She tried to scramble up, but she'd lost her slippers, and the ground was too slick for her to find purchase.

The taller man grabbed her arm and wrenched it behind her back, sending pain shooting through her shoulder. "Well, look what we have here," he said with a thin laugh. "You just made our job a little easier. Open the damn door."

"The police are on their way," Devan said, trying to infuse her voice with as much bravado as possible. Why hadn't she called 911 first? *Because they were about to break in. Because you didn't think.*

"Then we'll make this quick." Shoving her towards the door, he motioned to the other guy who'd retrieved the crowbar. "Let us in, and maybe you'll live through this."

"No," she said, trying to shake him off.

Her captor shifted, and the barrel of the gun pressed to her temple. "I won't ask you again, bitch."

Nausea soured her stomach. She was going to die. "I can't,"

she whispered. "I didn't bring my keys. I came down the back stairs." A single tear tumbled down her cheek.

"Fine. We'll do this the messy way," the larger man said, shoving her at his partner, who yanked her head back by her hair and wrapped his fingers around her throat.

With a firm kick to her deadbolt, the bigger guy sent her door swinging open. "Tie her up and gag her," he growled to his partner.

"Please...you don't have to do this," she begged, wheezing as she struggled to free herself. "Whatever he's...paying you...I'll... double it..." Not that she could, but they didn't know that.

Thug One rummaged around in his duffel bag and came away with a roll of duct tape. As he tore off a strip, Devan screamed and thrashed, but the fingers around her throat tightened, and she choked as the big man slapped the tape over her mouth. When he grabbed the belt from her robe and pulled it free, she used the man at her back as leverage, and kicked her feet out, catching Thug One in the groin.

"Fucking bitch!" he howled as he grabbed his nuts. "You'll pay for that."

Another kick behind her, and she loosened Thug Two's hold. Scrambling around the counter, she grabbed a five-pound bag of coffee and hurled it at Thug Two's head. He dodged just in time, and the bag exploded when it hit the ground, sending beans everywhere.

She dropped to her hands and knees as the gunshot exploded somewhere over her head. The mirror behind the counter shattered, and Devan covered her head with her hands as hundreds of shards rained down around her.

Blood slicked her fingers, and she clawed at the tape as she tried to shuffle forward on her knees. The panic button Mac had installed was only five feet away.

She managed to loosen the tape as the sound of a hammer being cocked over her head sent ice through her veins.

"Get up," the gunman growled.

A rough hand grasped her wrist and yanked, hard. But as she was jerked to her feet, she lunged for the panic button, her bloody fingers almost slipping off before she felt the subtle click.

Her captor dragged her over the counter and threw her against one of the tables. "Make it look good," he said to Thug Two as he advanced on Devan again.

With the crowbar, the shorter of her attackers smashed her pastry case, sending more glass skittering along the floor. "No!" Devan cried through the tape still half binding her lips. She grabbed the nearest chair, trying to use it to keep Thug One from coming any closer.

"Get the fuck away from her!" A blurry figure streaked into her shop, tackling the gunman and sending him to the ground. Devan blinked hard, her eyes watery, until Mac came into focus. He pummeled the thug, landing punch after punch to the man's head and gut.

Jerking the tape from her lips, she screamed, "Look out!"

Mac turned just in time to avoid taking a crowbar to his back and swept his leg out to catch the other thug's ankles. The man went down hard, and the crowbar clattered towards Devan.

She grabbed the weapon, swinging wildly, catching the gunman in the shoulder. He sank to his knees, and she brought the crowbar down a second time on his skull, knocking him out cold.

With one last uppercut, her rescuer—the man she'd ached to see for two days—laid Thug Two out on the floor of her shop. Mac got to his feet with the gun in his hand, wiping a drop of blood from his lip. His chest heaved and his shoulders slumped unevenly.

"Devan. Are you okay?" Wrapping his arms around her, he held her against the hard planes of his chest. The scent of him—fresh and clean—filled her nose, and she fisted his shirt, her hands shaking. Sirens blared, slowly getting louder.

When she didn't answer him, he grabbed a fistful of her hair and gently tipped her head back to look up at him. "Are you okay?" he asked again, more forcefully this time.

"Y-yes. I think...so..."

Mac's eyes narrowed. "You're bleeding."

"Mirror," she whispered as she buried her face against his chest. "I'm okay."

One of the thugs stirred. Mac whirled with Devan still held against him and leveled the gun at him. "Don't fucking move," he snapped. "Who hired you?"

The bruised and bloodied thug shook his head.

"Who?" Mac took a step closer, narrowing his gaze. "I'm in a hell of a lot of pain right now and you do not want to fuck with me. Answer the question."

"Some guy! I never saw him before. He knows Pete," the man said, gesturing towards the smaller thug who'd yet to regain consciousness. "Said he'd pay us a thousand bucks if we roughed her up and destroyed her shop. Kept going on about how she wouldn't listen."

"Sylvester," Devan whispered. "I was right."

The sirens were no more than a block away. Mac looked down at Devan. "Get my wallet out of my back pocket, sweetheart. Do it now."

"Why?"

"I need my military ID. They're going to frisk me and probably cuff me. I need you to go stand over there." He nodded his head towards the edge of the counter, not taking his eyes off the thugs. "Let the cops do their jobs. It'll all be okay."

Devan did what Mac told her, shivering from the cold and her dwindling adrenaline. Mac kept the gun pointed at the two thugs until the police car screeched to a halt and two officers burst into the shop.

"Hands in the air! Drop the gun!" One officer pointed his gun at Mac while the other headed for Devan.

Mac spun the gun and set it gingerly on the ground. He kicked it towards the officers and raised his arms, the ID in his left hand in plain view. "Retired Army Lieutenant Macdonald Fergerson. I'm...with Devan," he said, the briefest hitch in his voice. "This is my military ID card."

"Turn around and lace your hands behind your head."

"I'm injured." He turned, resting his right hand on the back of his head, but keeping his left held aloft. "I can't bend my left arm that way."

"Don't hurt him," Devan said. "They were going to destroy my shop. Mac stopped them. It's not his gun. It's theirs. I have cameras. They'll show everything."

The younger cop approached and kicked the crowbar away from Devan. The older one cuffed Mac's hands behind his back and pressed him against the wall. "Don't move."

"Mac?"

He grunted, pain knitting his brows and tightening lines around his eyes and mouth, but he offered her a wan smile. "Don't worry, sweetheart. I'm okay."

The two thugs were handcuffed and stowed in the back of the police car. Another unit showed up, and the first two cops on scene inquired about the cameras. Devan explained how to access the video feeds, and once the officers had confirmed Mac's story with the recorded video, the handcuffs were removed. He slumped against the counter, a few feet from Devan. One of the police officers, an older man named Officer Milton, asked about her previous trouble, and Devan told them all about Sylvester and her suspicions that he was behind the whole thing. The smaller of her two attackers—apparently the ringleader of the local gang who'd executed all of the attacks on Devan's shop—regained consciousness and confessed that they'd been hired by a man who described Devan as his 'no-good-sister'.

"Ma'am, you'll need to come down to the police station tomorrow and sign your formal statement, but we have enough to book these guys tonight. You and Lieutenant Fergerson are free to go. We've sent a unit to pick up your brother and we'll let you know what he says. In the meantime, I don't recommend you stay here tonight."

"She's staying with me." Mac pushed himself up and draped his right arm around Devan's shoulders, pulling her close.

Devan turned into the embrace, resting her cheek against his chest. Right now there wasn't anywhere else she wanted to be.

Mac led her upstairs and into her bathroom, cleaning and dressing a cut to the back of her hand and another on her left arm. "You don't need stitches," he said quietly, almost to himself. "Pack up what you need. Hammer and nails still in the office?"

Words seemed too hard, so she nodded, and Mac thudded down her stairs to secure her door while Devan grabbed a bag and shoved a change of clothes and her toothbrush inside. When Mac found her again, she was sitting on her couch, her head in her hands.

"Devan?"

She looked up at him, unsure what she needed but hoping he'd be able to figure it out.

Mac didn't speak, only pulled her to her feet and tucked her under his right arm. The walk to his building was silent, broken occasionally by a passing car or a faraway siren. Devan wasn't sure if Mac kept her close to protect her or to lean on her. His limp was worse than she'd ever seen it. "Bedroom's through there," he said when they'd made it inside, gesturing down the hall. "I'll take the couch."

Devan wanted him to stay with her, but the look he gave her said their sleeping arrangements weren't up for discussion. "Okay." As she pushed through the door, her eyes watered, but she swallowed hard, refusing to let herself cry.

The room fit him. A king-sized bed, done up in black and grays, a dark wood dresser and two matching nightstands. Everything was in order, the pillows arranged neatly on the bed, the closet door ajar, displaying half a dozen pairs of jeans and khakis, precisely folded t-shirts, waffle shirts, and one perfectly pressed military uniform.

Devan trailed her fingers along the thick bedspread. His scent filled the room, and she kicked off her boots, turned off the light, and huddled under the blankets. After tossing and turning for a few minutes, she grabbed a second pillow and hugged it to her chest.

She didn't remember falling asleep, but she woke to Mac's hands on her, pulling her against him while he buried his face in her curls.

"Mac?"

"Tell me to leave," he said, his voice hoarse in her ear.

"Stay."

a shaft of sunlight woke him, and the scents of eggs, butter, and coffee wafted in from the kitchen. Shit. He'd slept half the night. Without drugs. With Devan in his bed. In his arms.

He'd tried to stay away. Tried to give her space. But every time he closed his eyes, he saw her on the floor, bleeding, a piece of duct tape half-gagging her. And then, from his bedroom, she'd whimpered. Only once. A bad dream, perhaps. But the sound had shattered him.

Her scent soothed something deep inside him. He wanted her in his bed every night. But, he couldn't get his hopes up until he showed her exactly what she was getting herself into.

Devan hummed "Silent Night" as she scrambled eggs, and scones cooled on a rack next to the stove.

"How long have you been up?" Mac asked.

The wooden spoon in her hand clattered to the countertop and she pressed her hand to her chest. "You scared me."

In three steps, he was at her side and brushed a knuckle along her cheek. "You're exhausted. You didn't need to cook."

"I'm too much of a morning person," she said quietly. "And I had to do...something. I...my shop..."

"Shhh, sweetheart. It's going to be okay." Mac wrapped his arms around her, and she tucked her head under his chin. As her hand stroked down the left side of his back, he tried not to pull away. "This smells amazing. Let's eat."

Devan shuddered as extricated herself from his embrace. "You hardly had anything for me to work with. The scones are probably going to suck. But at least the coffee's good."

For the next ten minutes, the silence was only broken by the scraping of forks against plates and sips of coffee. After Devan had cleared the plates away, Mac took her hand and pulled her into the bedroom.

"Mac?" With her brown eyes wide and a tremble to her voice, Devan let him ease her down onto the bed. "Talk to me."

"I didn't think I'd be in time. Last night." Mac rubbed the back of his neck, staring down at his feet. "I almost lost you."

"I'm—"

Mac held up his hand. "I don't want to hide anymore, Devan. But...you have to know...I'm damaged goods. Seriously fucked up."

"Do you think I care?" She reached for his hands, linking their fingers and holding on tight. "You saved my life, Mac. And even if you'd never needed to...I like you. A lot. You're...infuriating, overprotective, and closed-off. But you're also capable, talented, and funny—when you're not hiding behind whatever it is you're so afraid of."

Mac stripped off his long-sleeved t-shirt, carefully watching Devan's face for any reaction. She rose, the corners of her lips curving slightly. "Will it hurt if I touch you?"

"It'll hurt more if you don't." The admission cost him, and his shoulders slumped as Devan fluttered her fingers over his left shoulder.

"Tell me." She traced the staple scars, leaned in, and kissed the roughened patch of skin along his side.

"We were on a routine patrol. The mortar hit our transpo, and the whole vehicle flipped and rolled down an embankment. Terry was thrown clear, but I was dazed. It took me a minute to get my bearings. When the second mortar hit, I was only a foot away from the engine. The shrapnel came from everywhere."

Devan ran her hands over his chest, down his arms. "Keep going." When she reached the waistband of his fleece pants, he stiffened and closed his eyes.

Naked in front of her, he struggled to find his next words. "I thought I was dead. Until I heard Terry screaming. Dragged myself over to him and wrapped a tourniquet around his leg to stop him from bleeding out."

Devan circled him, touching every scar. Every patch of burned, seared skin, the angry red lines that streaked across his back. "Look at me, Mac."

When he met her gaze, she was smiling. And on her knees. With her hands wrapped around his hips, she drew him closer, and traced her tongue over the indentation along the top of his hip where the doctors had removed part of the bone.

With a lick of her lips, she took the tip of his cock in her mouth, her gaze meeting his for permission. He could only manage a single nod, then a groan as she took him deep, swirling her tongue around the head of his cock and down over the thick vein.

"Shit. Devan." He tightened his fingers in her hair, guiding her movements, unable to stop himself from falling in love with this maddening and beautiful woman before him. Light danced in her warm brown eyes as she sucked and licked, reaching up to cup his balls. Her other hand never left the scarred skin of his ass, and she gripped him firmly enough to hold him to her, but not so hard that she'd hurt him.

A tingle started in his toes and worked its way up through his legs. He couldn't hold on much longer. "Devan...I'm going to...fuck."

When she purred, the sensation carried him over the edge, and his hips bucked as he spilled himself into her with such force, his knees threatened to buckle.

She swallowed and drew her lips around his spent cock, releasing him with a gentle kiss. After getting to her feet, Devan wrapped her arms around his naked body. "I see you, Mac. And I'm not running." Her hand trailed up his six-pack and brushed his right nipple and he shuddered. "I want to know every inch of you."

"You'll stay?"

"I'll stay."

Mac scooped her up, ignoring the ache in his shoulder, and laid her on the bed. Crawling up next to her, he pinned her wrists to the mattress. "If you're going to stay, these clothes...have to go."

"Oh really?" She smiled, a light laugh tripping from her lips. God, he loved that sound. The depth of emotion welling in her eyes. "Take me, Mac. I'm yours."

EPILOGUE

Christmas Eve, Devan opened the shop at 8:00 a.m. At nine, heavy footsteps clomping down her back stairs brought a smile to her face. Mac came in, his hair still damp from the shower. "You left."

"I told you I had to open for a few hours," she replied.

"Besides, you looked so cute in my bed."

He grabbed one of her bar towels and threw it at her. "I'm not cute."

"No. Of course not. You're ruggedly handsome and strong." *And incredibly cute when you're sleeping amid a purple comforter and pink body pillow.*

They'd been practically inseparable at night since Mac had shown her his scars. During the day, they both worked—her at Artist's Grind, him at the metal shop—but at night, they always came back together.

A corner of her shop now boasted an assortment of his metal Christmas trees, picture frames, and candle holders. Business cards were stacked neatly in a metal tray, and the sales had boosted his confidence enough for him to take pieces around to some of the other local shops and galleries in town.

"Pies in the walk-in?" Mac asked.

"Yep. Cookies too." In two hours, they'd be in Mac's truck on their way to Vermont to spend the rest of Christmas Eve and part of Christmas Day with Terry and his sister's family. Nerves tightened in her belly as she thought about the little box tucked in her purse wrapped in silver paper. It wasn't much. One of Elora's rings, sized for his thumb. But stamped on the inside, were the words "For the man I love."

She wished she'd been able to do more. But in the ten days since the attack, she'd had to coordinate all the repairs for her shop as well as file formal charges against Sylvester.

Her half-brother was in so much hot water, she'd entertained dropping her suit against him, but Mac begged her to reconsider. "He hurt you, sweetheart. Please. Do this for me." He asked for so little, she'd agreed immediately.

The bells over the door jingled as Mac pressed a kiss to the back of her neck. A well-dressed man in a long, leather coat crossed the threshold, moving stiffly. Devan's mouth fell open. Alexander Fairhaven. A member of Boston's royal elite—if the city had royalty—walked in with his girlfriend, Elizabeth Bennett, at his side. A few days earlier, Elizabeth had visited the shop and left with a handful of gifts—including some of Mac's pieces.

"Happy Christmas," he said with a genuine smile and a refined British accent.

"Merry Christmas," Devan replied.

Elizabeth approached the counter while Alexander perused the shop. "Do you still have the beans from the other day? The Peruvian?" When Devan nodded, she grinned. "Two pour-overs to go, please. And one of those cranberry scones."

"Right away."

While Devan made the coffee, Mac slid a scone into a paper bag and handed it to Elizabeth. When she headed to Alexander's side, Mac leaned down and whispered in Devan's ear, "You know her?"

"She came in the other day."

"This is brilliant," Alexander said, gesturing to the metal work. "Do you know if the artist—" he picked up one of Mac's cards, "—has larger pieces?"

"Mac?" Devan grinned and looked to the man she'd fallen in love with. "Do you have larger pieces?"

Alexander's eyes lit up. "You made this?"

"It's lovely," Elizabeth said, fingering the burnished iron. "Truly."

"I'd like to talk to you further. Not on Christmas Eve, of course. Elizabeth and I have somewhere to be. May I ring you after the new year? I need a new piece for Fairhaven's corporate offices. We're redoing the executive floor in January."

"Uh, yeah. Sure. That would be great," Mac stammered.

Alexander paid for the coffees and the scone, leaving a twenty-dollar tip, and they slipped back out the door, disappearing into the snow.

Devan and Mac looked at each other for a minute before she launched herself into his arms. "The richest man in Boston wants to buy your art."

"I..." Mac held her close and buried his face in her hair. "I love you, Devan. I know it's soon, but it's Christmas Eve. And without you, I'd be alone in my apartment, feeling sorry for myself. You've changed me. Falling in love with you has changed me."

"I love you, too," she replied softly. "Merry Christmas, Mac."

* * *

DEAR READER,

Mac was one of the first military heroes who told me his story.

Since then, I've spent time with Garrett, Cam, Royce, West, Inara, and Ryker. And then there are Dax, Ripper, Terry, and Nomar. Their stories are still to come. These broken men and women are special to me. Whether they're scarred, suffering from PTSD, or are simply unused to functioning in a normal society after years of war, they're strong and vulnerable at the same time.

That's why these characters speak to me. I think we're all a little broken inside. But my definition of broken isn't the norm. I think broken can be beautiful. In fact, I think broken can be even *more* beautiful than perfection.

I hope you'll continue reading my military romance books. Next, let Garrett and Lilah take you to Seattle for Valentine's Day in **_Love and Libations_**. An amputee bartender meets a woman who's been told over and over again that she's nothing.

But to Garrett, Lilah is everything.

Thank you for reading.

Love,

Patricia

<<<<>>>>

ABOUT THE AUTHOR

I've always made up stories. Sometimes I even acted them out. I probably shouldn't admit that my childhood best friend and I used to run around the backyard pretending to fly in our Invisible Jet and rescue Steve Trevor. Oops.

Now that I'm too old to spin around in circles with felt magic bracelets on my wrists, I put "pen to paper" instead. Figuratively, at least. Fingers to keyboard is more accurate.

Outside of my writing, I'm a professional editor, a software geek, a singer (in the shower only), and a runner. I love red wine, scotch (neat, please), and cider. Seattle is my home, and I share an old house with my husband and cats.

I'm on my fourth—fifth?—rewatching of the modern *Doctor Who*, and I think one particular quote from that show sums up my entire life.

"We're all stories, in the end. Make it a good one, eh?" — *The Eleventh Doctor, Doctor Who*

I hope your story is brilliant.

facebook.com/patriciadeddyauthor

twitter.com/patriciadeddy

instagram.com/patriciadeddy

ALSO BY PATRICIA D. EDDY

By the Fates

Check out the By the Fates series if you love dark and steamy tales of witches, devils, and an epic battle between good and evil.

By the Fates, Freed

Destined, a By the Fates Story

By the Fates, Fought

By the Fates, Fulfilled

* * *

In Blood

If you love hot Italian vampires and and a human who can hold her own against beings far stronger, then the In Blood series is for you.

Secrets in Blood

Revelations in Blood

* * *

Elemental Shifter

Hot werewolves and strong, powerful elementals. What's not to love?

A Shift in the Water

A Shift in the Air

* * *

Contemporary and Erotic Romances

Holidays and Heroes

Beauty isn't only skin deep and not all scars heal. Come swoon over sexy vets and the men and women who love them.

Mistletoe and Mochas

Love and Libations

* * *

Away From Keyboard

Dive into a steamy mix of geekery and military might with the men and women of Emerald City Security and Hidden Agenda Services.

Breaking His Code

In Her Sights

On His Six

* * *

Restrained

Do you like to be tied up? Or read about characters who do? Enjoy a fresh BDSM series that will leave you begging for more.

In His Silks

Christmas Silks

All Tied Up For New Year's

In His Collar

Made in the USA
Middletown, DE
18 March 2020